ROAD TRIP TO
PASSION

ROAD TRIP TO
PASSION

SAHARA KELLY

LANI AAMES

VONNA HARPER

POCKET BOOKS

NEW YORK   LONDON   TORONTO   SYDNEY

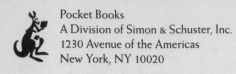

Pocket Books
A Division of Simon & Schuster, Inc.
1230 Avenue of the Americas
New York, NY 10020

First Pocket Books trade paperback edition February 2008

POCKET and colophon are registered trademarks of Simon & Schuster, Inc.

For information about special discounts for bulk purchases, please contact Simon & Schuster Special Sales at 1-800-456-6798 or business@simonandscuster.com.

Manufactured in the United States of America

10 9 8 7 6 5 4 3 2 1

Library of Congress Cataloging-in-Publication Data

Road trip to passion / Sahara Kelly, Lani Aames, Vonna Harper.—1st
Pocket Books trade pbk. ed.
    p.   cm. — (Ellora's Cave anthologies)
    1. Erotic stories, American. I. Kelly, Sahara. Anasazi lassie. II. Aames, Lani.
Statuesque. III. Harper, Vonna. Night of the cougar.

PS648.E7R63 2008
813'.60803538—dc22   2007047426

ISBN-13: 978-1-4165-7662-4
ISBN-10:   1-4165-7662-2

CONTENTS

ANASAZI
LASSIE

SAHARA KELLY

ONE

"I REALLY DON'T THINK THIS is a very good idea . . ."

Marjorie Hayworth struggled with her suitcase and whined. No doubt about it, it was a definite, not-to-be-confused-with-a-passing-comment *whine*.

"*Can* it, Midge. You're going and that's all there is to it." Professor Jen Peterson glared at Marjorie as if challenging her to respond with yet another whine.

"But . . ."

The word had scarcely passed her lips when her chairwoman whirled around and stuck her hands on her hips in a very un-academic pose. "Marjorie Hayworth, you are the most qualified researcher I have available for this project. It's taken you quite a bit of time to set up a visit for *anybody* from our department to go to the Tolikani Canyon site. Your knowledge and published papers helped enormously when it came to dealing with those historical authorities who guard that place like it's Fort Knox or something. Who the fuck else *would* I send?"

"Er . . . Dan Mitchell?"

Jen snorted. "That twit? He doesn't know a potsherd from a goatherd and God forbid he be forced to camp *outside*."

Marjorie nodded agreement. It had been the first name that had popped into her head since Dan had invited her to the faculty tea next week. At least this trip spared her *that* particular agony.

"Jen, you know I'm *not* a fieldwork person. I much prefer doing research in the library or online . . ."

"Too bad. Time you got out into the fresh air and got your hands dirty." To say that Professor Peterson gloated would be overstating things. There was, however, a distinct gleam of mischief in those crinkled eyes.

Marjorie sighed, accepting the inevitable.

"You might just enjoy it, Midge. Honestly. Sunshine, the chance to poke around the site, pick up stuff firsthand . . . some folks would kill for that opportunity."

"It'll probably kill *me* . . ." Marjorie mumbled her response under her breath as she lugged her old suitcase to the side of the bus and watched the driver stow it away in the bowels of their transportation.

"Ah. Here's the rest of the party." Jen turned and watched several people, also carrying luggage, stroll toward the bus.

"Oh *goody*."

With a clear lack of enthusiasm, Marjorie looked at her fellow travelers. It was her worst nightmare combined with every horrid experience she'd ever imagined, all rolled into one.

Smiling happily was the beautiful and very blonde Shawna Adams. Shawna was studying Art History and specializing in Southwest styles. She wouldn't be coming to the site itself, but her thesis advisor had wangled her a seat on this trip. It saved him money and probably also saved his marriage, since there'd been a rumor or two about how Shawna kept her grades as high as her hemline.

Both were inappropriately stratospheric, in Marjorie's opinion. But then again, when you were twenty-two and built like the proverbial brick shithouse, it probably didn't matter how short you wore your skirts.

Absently she tugged at the waistband of her practical cargo pants and felt to make sure the top button on her denim shirt was fastened at her neck. Not that anyone would notice what a just-turned-thirty Assistant Professor with mousy brown hair was wearing.

Least of all Webster Jones.

Professor Webster Jones. Greenhill College's answer to the more famous "Dr. Jones" of movie fame. Some students had even nicknamed him "Indiana," but he'd shot that down rapidly, saying he was from Massachusetts which did not, in any way shape or form, go well with "Jones." Nor did he have a dog named "Indiana."

The tag persisted though. And the way he looked was certainly in keeping with Hollywood's idea of a leading man.

Because Web Jones had been blessed with just about every attribute from a maiden's dream along with a few from the dreams of non-maidens as well.

Marjorie sighed as she contemplated the idea of a day's bus ride with Web Jones. She couldn't help one or two visions of hot and sweaty sex in the rear seat, but they were fleeting and very definitely unrealistic.

First off, the seats were probably imitation plastic and would get uncomfortable pretty damn quick. Then there was the business of managing assorted limbs into positions that would ensure bliss. And of course there was also *having* that bliss.

Web probably knew how. Marjorie didn't. *Bliss* hadn't been part of her limited sexual experiences.

Finally of course, there was the one insurmountable obstacle to all these lovely little fantasies—Web didn't know she existed. They'd passed like the proverbial ships in the night, but with latitudes so separate that they'd been too far away to even toot their horns. He was in the English department—a professor of journalism—and her Archaeology department was on the other side of campus. While his reputation spread like ripples on an ocean of feminine yearnings, her reputation didn't warrant a splatter from a mud puddle.

She didn't actually *have* a reputation. For *anything*. Which was, in and of itself, appallingly depressing.

Web was writing a book—a novel of all things—and he wanted to get some firsthand knowledge of the setting. Apparently that setting placed his characters in the Southwest, in some past time, perhaps around the time of her own particular fascination—the Anasazi.

Marjorie sighed. The truth of the matter was that her heart lay not in the current goings-on in her academic faculty environment, but in the past. Some thousand years in the past, when a civilization had lived and died and left a mystery behind them to plague future scholars—like Marjorie.

What had happened to the Anasazi? And why? And the most important question of all—who were they and how did they live? What were their lives like in their cleverly constructed houses built into the steep walls of canyons? Who did they worship in their subterranean religious structures called *kivas*?

This particular culture seemed defined more by what historians *didn't* know than by what they did know. To Marjorie, it was a source of endless fascination. Their story had seized her imagination when she'd first read of them, probably played a good sized role in directing her feet onto the path of archaeology and resulted in her current trip to a deserted little corner of the southwest United States. A chance to touch what was theirs, to see what they saw and to breathe the air they may have breathed.

A gust of bus fumes soured her nose and made her cough.

Okay. So the breathing thing might be a bit different, since the air had definitely deteriorated over the past thousand years.

"Ready?" Jen pushed Marjorie toward the bus.

"Would it matter if I said no?"

"Nope." Marjorie's boss and good friend grinned. "Have a lovely time. Find lots of artifacts. Soak up the atmosphere. Write many wonderful award-winning papers. Make me look good."

In spite of her apprehension about this trip, Marjorie couldn't help grinning back. "Don't I always?"

Then, with her heart in her sturdy hiking boots, she climbed up the small mountain of stairs into the belly of her transportation.

They were off.

IT WAS THE HEAT that finished her off.

The nervous week she'd endured making sure all the details were in place, combined with the necessity of packing for herself and making her own personal arrangements had exhausted her.

Midge was tired and realized it as soon as her ass hit the warm seat. Now it was all out of her hands and she could relax.

Her laptop was next to her, along with a small pile of folders she intended to review on the way. But her attention was distracted by Shawna, whose mile-long legs seemed to be on an eternal stroll up and down the aisle of the bus. Nobody should be allowed to have legs that perfect, decided Midge. It was just too damned unfair.

Of course, if she'd happened to possess legs like that, she might have shown them off to the world in general as well. Certainly the bus driver appreciated the sight, since one of his rearview mirrors seemed angled to give him a super crotch shot every time Shawna sat down in the front seat and crossed her legs. Which she did, quite a few times.

Then there was Web. To give him his due, he did not plant himself next to Shawna and seduce her panties off. It wouldn't have taken much seducing either, in Midge's admittedly biased and bitchy opinion.

No, Web had his own laptop open a couple of seats in front of Midge across the aisle. She could see the sun dappling fingers of light across his black hair now and again. Rather like she wanted to, come to think of it.

Midge blinked and yawned. Foolishly, she'd selected a seat that took the full force of the sun as it rose. Even though the windows were made of filtered and tinted glass, it was hot. What air-conditioning there was didn't seem to penetrate into Midge's little corner of the world and she quietly unfastened a couple of buttons and fanned her throat with a notepad.

There was little to see outside—their trip would last most of the day and get them to their destination around sunset, give or take. The highway carved a trail through deserted wilderness, lying hotly in the sunshine, offering nothing much in the way of scenic distraction.

In the distance a purple band on the horizon told of mountains sleeping peacefully, but as yet, it was all dust and the occasional small town. As the day got hotter, even the mountains would disappear into the shimmer of the haze.

Midge leaned her head back on the seat and decided it would be okay to close her eyes for a few moments. She could review her plans. After they arrived and the others were settled in the only motel around for miles, she hoped to walk the short distance from there to the actual site. There was a simple campground, set up by the original discoverers of this place. *That* was where Midge wanted to be.

Surrounded by the mysteries of the desert, the uncluttered expanse of space and time, the quiet of a night where the stars were huge and magic . . . all the wonderful things she'd imagined before falling asleep in her tidy little college apartment.

And she dreamed . . .

Midge dreamed of a man. Anasazi most probably, since his hair was long, a black ribbon of shining silk down his spine, unbound and beautiful. His cheekbones were strong, his eyes . . . *mmm*, those were eyes a woman could drown in, willingly.

He was standing on the very top of a mesa, backed by clouds reflecting the sun as it rose. Purple, red and orange flames caressed the billows behind him and he held out his hand to Midge.

"Come watch with me."

She found herself rising, walking toward his outstretched arm, a heat within her stoked higher by the look he gave her body.

Her naked body.

Somewhere in Midge a voice shrieked and was quickly smothered. This was a dream. She knew it and accepted it as such. Her scruples could take the day off.

"It's beautiful, isn't it?" His voice was sexy, as sexy as the rest of him and Midge found herself standing straighter, thrusting her breasts forward, pulling her shoulders back and relishing the knowledge that he was *hers*. "Yes. Yes, it is."

His arms circled her waist and he pulled her against him, her back to his front. Yes, he was naked too. Why the hell hadn't she checked the rest of him out instead of losing herself in his eyes? Midge gave herself a solid mental kick up the ass, only to suck in a breath as something *else* poked her in the ass.

A real solid length of masculinity was snuggled against her as he held her tightly. "I shall take you soon. When the sun has risen and I can see all of you as I claim you."

Midge cleared her throat. "Er . . . you will?"

"Oh yes, my little one. Did you think that I could ever let you go after just one taste?"

"You tasted me?" Damn frickin' dreams. Always started *after* the good parts.

"Your lips are sweet, Midge. I want to taste all of you. I want to drown in your juices, to make them flow as freely as the waters after the rain bathes the mountaintops."

Midge thought about that. *Briefly.* "Okay."

"And I want to hear you scream louder than the eagle. I want you to scream my name as you voyage to look the

Goddess in the face and return to my arms. And I shall travel with you."

Midge swallowed. "Good to know."

"You will scream, my sweet one. You will scream until the name *Ashiike* fills the valleys and the gorges."

Midge blinked. "That means boy." She wrinkled her nose. "In Navajo. I think."

"Are you in any doubt that I am male?" The laughing question was accompanied by an extra-strong thrust of his hips and the simultaneous cupping of her breasts. "I am in no doubt that you are female, my Midge. No doubt whatsoever."

Strong fingers played with her nipples, arousing them to hard and sensitive buds that he stroked delicately. Little darts of exquisite fire shot directly to her cunt without passing go, collecting any money whatsoever, or even asking permission.

Under his skilled caresses, Midge went from zero to *almost-coming* in about point seven seconds flat.

She sighed and moved her feet a little, parting her thighs in what was—for her—a shameless and wanton invitation. Her breasts were heating under the rays of the emerging sun and the attentions of Ashiike, swelling into his palms as he kneaded, squeezed and played with her.

She *hurt*, aching for more of his touches, especially in the place that was now busily preparing for new adventures that might involve the insertion and removal of assorted gender-specific body parts.

Midge blinked. What *was* the matter with her? She was about to get thoroughly seduced by a super-gorgeous dream Anasazi warrior. It was a time for panting and nibbling and fucking—not analysis or scientific observation.

The universe swirled around her as he swept her off her feet and into his arms. "It's time."

"Oh good." She breathed in a unique fragrance—manly, tangy and yet sweet. Like cinnamon or sage or something. She'd never been much use at identifying scents. But this one—well, it would be forever identified with Ashiike in her olfactory lobes.

Something soft met her spine and she realized she was lying on a skin, some sort of deer or bison perhaps. Part of her wanted to take a look at it, classify it and make notes. The rest of her was blinded by the sunrise and the man looming over her. His chest was a work of art, his face intense as he gazed at her body. Muscles knotted his arms as he positioned himself between her legs, which she obligingly parted to make room. Nothing said she couldn't help out this dream lover, right?

He wore a small band of beads around one shining biceps, which distracted Midge. She knew she wanted to look at the rest of him. To touch, to feel—to fully experience this magnificent *claiming* she was about to enjoy. So why was she staring at these beads? Noting the turquoise and the white design?

Her pussy was swollen and wet—she could feel the folds throbbing as they anticipated Ashiike and his cock. He was groaning as he settled himself, sighing with pleasure as his hands skimmed her hips, positioning her where he wanted her, snuggling himself into the vee of her thighs.

There—she felt it. The head of his cock, velvety against her moisture, slicking around, rooting for the entrance to paradise.

She closed her eyes for a second, relishing the sensation. Then she opened them once more. This was a time for enjoying every moment, for watching his every move, not hiding within her private physical responses.

It was a time for—sharing, feeling, loving—for opening herself to him and blooming under his touch like a rose in the desert.

Midge huffed out a breath of irritation. It was also *no* time for stupid hyperbole, so she needed to just shut up her brains and let her body take over. She stared up at Ashiike and found inspiration to do just that.

His eyes were burning, red lights shining from behind dark irises. Whether it was the sunlight or what, Midge had no idea, but as his cock sank past her pussy and into her cunt, his eyes definitely flamed with heat.

And as he pulled back and made ready to penetrate her once more, she saw his features shift—change slightly into something more familiar.

"Holy *shit*." She opened her mouth just as he plunged deeply inside her and hit her clit dead on target. "*Web!*"

The scream strangled in her throat and she choked, waking to find herself sprawled across two seats, bouncing around as the bus hit a pocket of turbulently bad road surface.

Her weighty backpack had fallen into her lap and her water bottle was abrading her crotch in the most delightfully stimulating of ways. She would have simply let nature take its course but for one rather annoying detail.

Web Jones was leaning over the seat in front of her and staring down into her eyes. "You called?"

Oh *fuck*.

TWO

*D*R. WEB JONES WAS enjoying himself enormously.

He was out of the occasionally stifling academic environment and on his way to breath some real outdoor air into lungs that felt starved now and again. His novel was coming together really well, needing only the touch of reality his visit to this particular area would bring.

He'd felt "called" by this tale as soon as he'd stumbled on the legend of the Anasazi, much as he imagined Marjorie Hayworth had been "called." She certainly seemed to be enthusiastic on the subject, to judge by the lectures he'd dropped in to hear.

Sneaking quietly into the back of the room, he'd watched her mobile expressions, observed her passion for the past and become entranced by the flashes of sensual beauty that shone from her face as she'd let herself go, falling into the pleasure of sharing her interests with her recitation section.

He saw beneath the staid and proper façade of the Assistant Professor. He saw past the trappings of denim and khaki and sensible shoes. He saw the curves, he saw the heat and he saw the *woman*.

He just hadn't had the chance to do much about it until this trip popped up on his radar and he jumped at the opportunity to kill two birds with one stone. Sort of. Or at least to kill one bird and get a shot at making out with the other one.

The one who was, at this particular moment, glaring at him from her tangle of limbs, clothing and luggage. Since her face was flushed and her thighs were wrapped around her backpack, it didn't require the analytical mind of an Einstein to figure out what she'd been dreaming about.

Web grinned. "Anything I can do?"

She frowned. "No. Go away."

"Can't. It goes against my upbringing to ignore a lady in distress. And you did call my name . . ."

Marjorie slithered around and straightened her clothing, sweat beading her forehead and damp spots darkening the shirt around her armpits. "I did not."

"Did too. I heard you." He took pity on her and offered a fresh bottle of cold water he'd grabbed from the cooler they'd stashed on the bus. "Here. You look thirsty."

"Observant of you." Wryly, she curled her lip but accepted the bottle all the same, swigging down a healthy swallow and then touching the cool surface to her cheeks. "God, it's hot."

"That's what happens when you fall asleep in the sunshine of the desert Southwest."

"Thank you, Mr. I-live-to-state-the-obvious."

"Oooh. *Somebody* woke up in a bad mood. Must have been a pretty awful dream, huh?" Web snickered at Marjorie.

She impaled him with a look of absolute disgust. "Thank you for the water. Will there be anything else?"

"Dunno." He slipped from the seat in front of her to the seat beside her, pushing stuff onto the floor without a second thought.

"Hey." Outraged, Marjorie dived for her laptop. "*Watch it. That's precious cargo.*"

"Sorry." Web knew he didn't sound sorry. He wasn't sorry anyway. He didn't give a hoot about her laptop. He was where he wanted to be and the scent of this hot woman was making him a little light-headed.

It was a nice light-headed—the sort of light-headed one got just before stripping and fucking—for hours on end . . .

The sharp jab of a metallic computer corner in his ribs jerked Web from his idyllic visions. "Ouch."

"Sorry." This time it was her turn to snicker and look unrepentant.

He rubbed his side. "So you're really going to go and grub among the ruins?"

She fidgeted and fussed some more, finally getting her belongings where she wanted them. "I wouldn't describe scientific investigation as grubbing, but yes, I plan on doing a little digging while we're at Tolikani Canyon." She raised an eyebrow at him. "Don't worry. I won't be asking you to do any. This is a job for those who know what they're doing."

"Ouch again."

To give her credit, she looked abashed. "Yeah, that was a pretty horrid comment. I'm sorry, Dr. Jones. I guess that nap really didn't help much. I seem to be in a rather unpleasant mood. Perhaps you should go . . ."

"Call me Web."

"Huh?"

"Web. It's a damn sight better than Webster. I can't abide the *Dr. Jones* thing. Too . . ."

"Lost ark?"

He sighed. "And *then* some."

"Web it is." She held out her hand. "And I'm Midge."

He took it, noting the delicately long fingers, a surprise when contrasted to the sturdy image she presented at first glance. "Midge? Like the gnat?"

She sighed in her turn. "Look. Here's the deal. I won't do any Dr. Jones jokes if you don't do any insect jokes. Okay?"

He chuckled and squeezed her hand, surprising himself and her by bringing it to his lips and dropping a courtly kiss on the knuckles. "It's a deal, Midge."

He was pleased to note how she responded—a moment's shocked stillness followed by a blush and a definite increase in her scent.

Why he could smell her so clearly, he had no idea. She wasn't in need of a shower, nor was she drenched with perfume or lotions. The fragrance was all *her*—woman, heat, the desert sun and a soft sweetness that bloomed from her body in a mix of musk and flowers that had no name. It found a home in his nostrils, curled its way into his memories and from there proceeded to trot down his spinal column into his groin where it tapped his cock politely on the shoulder and woke it from a sound sleep.

He shifted position a little, easing the growing tension in his jeans. "You know, we should probably have Indian names for this trip."

She pulled her hand free and cleared her throat. "You mean like in kindergarten? Walks-with-two-dogs? Things like that?"

"Mine was Runs-with-scissors."

Her laugh was a delight, ringing out heartily and making the driver's head lift to check his mirror. Shawna was sleeping in the front two seats, legs splayed wide in the heat of the midday sun. The driver spent about a microsecond looking at Web and Midge. The bus swerved then pulled back onto a straight course as he got a clear pussy shot up Shawna's skirt.

Web shook his head. "I sure hope that guy can get us to Tolikani in one piece."

Midge had obviously noted the same things Web had. "If he can keep his eyes on the road and off Shawna's crotch, we stand a good chance of arriving safely."

"Hmm."

"Not that any man could be expected to exert *that* much control . . ." Midge was trying hard not to stare at Shawna. "She's just a walking distraction, isn't she?"

"For some men, I suppose."

"Yes. The ones with a pulse."

"Don't be too hard on us. We're simple creatures at heart." Web managed a wounded look.

"Indeed. Like amoebas with a single goal."

"To bring our mates pleasure." He lifted a hand and brushed an errant lock of hair back behind her ear.

She blinked, dipped her head and shot him a self-conscious glance from beneath her eyelashes. It was a simple thing, but one that shot straight to his crotch. She had no idea whatsoever how sexy it was.

"Ah, my *Ma'ay*."

"What?"

Web straightened, surprised at himself. "Uh . . . it means fox in Navajo. You just . . . the way you looked at me . . ." He swallowed. "Look, I do apologize. I'm not getting fresh here . . ." *The hell I'm not.*

"You speak Navajo?" She hadn't squirmed into the far corner of the seat, which was a good thing Web supposed.

"No, *God no.* Far too complex a language for a mere mortal to speak." He smiled at her, doing his best to radiate charm and non-threatening friendship. "But I have a relative who does. He speaks quite a few languages, does Uncle Eddie."

"Really? Is he an archaeologist?"

"Nope. Works for the government. He's the one who told me about the Anasazi a long time ago and probably got this novel of mine started somewhere in my cerebral cortex. He's not really my uncle by blood, just a family friend."

"How neat. To know somebody who actually speaks Navajo, like the Code Talkers."

"Yeah." Web nodded, knowing she was referring to the World War II units manned by Navajos whose language was transformed into an unbreakable code. "Pretty impressive. But then, so were the Anasazi from what I've read and learned." He leaned back and lifted one foot to rest the heel on the seat in front.

He couldn't miss her quick glance at his lap or the way her throat moved when she swallowed. There was something innately fascinating about this woman, besides her scent and Web was determined to figure out what it was. She was sexy, earthy, sensual, in an appealingly innocent way and pretty much totally unaware of any of the above.

Perhaps therein lay her charm.

"The Anasazi . . . oh yes. They were impressive." She stared out of the window and Web was struck with the fanciful notion that she was looking into the past rather than at the passing scenery. "A well-developed society, skilled crafters and builders, a solid religious component—and then they were just *gone*. Disappeared in what was practically the blink of an archeological eye."

"And you want to know why." It was a statement not a question.

"Of course. But I'd like to know how they lived more than why they died. I'd like to know what they thought, how they loved, who they worshipped—all that sort of stuff."

Absently, Midge tugged her shirt collar apart and brushed away a couple of droplets of sweat. More rolled down into the abundant cleavage she'd unthinkingly revealed.

Web gulped and forced himself to concentrate on her words not her breasts. "They were people, Midge. Just like us but without the cell phones."

She looked back at him, all mussed hair and blue-purple eyes. Why hadn't he noticed her eyes before now? They were the color of some flower or other. Not quite violet, but not a pure blue either. The bus around him disappeared for an instant as he fell into the depths of those eyes.

Then she spoke and he surfaced, shaken to his core.

"You really think they were just like us?"

It took a second for the words to become intelligible to Web, since his head was still whirling from his brief trip into some sensual fantasy. "Yes. I think they were just like us."

I know they were like us. I've seen them in my dreams.

And I've seen you in my dreams too.

Naked.

Midge worked on her laptop, seemingly ignoring him, letting his words drift off in the dust left behind by the bus. Whether she was actually unaware of him or not, didn't really matter.

Web just relaxed and indulged himself, remembering his most recent dream.

It was dark, the total darkness of a wild and uncivilized place, soft air around them and soft grass beneath them.

He'd chased her across what seemed like miles of emptiness, her laughter a temptation that lured him on. She was quick, quicker than the creatures he hunted—or at least he felt she was.

Their feet made little sound and he could hear her quick breaths along with the rise and fall of her hair as it tumbled around her.

She would let him catch her. He always caught her. This time it would be atop the world instead of next to a river or beneath massive rock outcroppings that had stood since time began. It didn't matter if she was tall or short, dark or fair—she was *his*.

The band of beads around his biceps throbbed as his blood thundered through his veins, the thought of taking her, claiming her, driving his heart to beat like the drums that sounded at dawn before a hunt began.

Finally, she slowed her pace, stopping—as he had anticipated—on the very top of the rise. She turned, her teeth a flash of white in the darkness.

"You are slow tonight, Ashiike." She taunted him, laughter in her voice.

"I must conserve some strength, Ma'ay. I shall need it to make you scream out my name to the skies." He came up beside her and stood there, letting her scent fill him and arouse him to near-painful hardness.

She hunched a shoulder and turned away. "What makes you think I shall permit you to take me?"

He slid his hands around her, finding her nipples beaded beneath the necklaces she wore. "These." He pinched them.

"Ow." She let out a little yip but did not pull away.

He kept one hand toying with a breast while the other slipped beneath her loincloth. "And *this* . . ." His fingers sought and found the heat of her desire, wet and slippery folds of flesh hiding the taut bud he knew so well.

"Ahhh . . ." She sighed as he slid a finger into her cunt. "Yes, my Ashiike. I think I will let you take me."

"As *you* shall take *me*. All of me." He let his hand fall away from her breast and found the ties to her garment. It dropped to the grass, followed quickly by his own.

This was how they were meant to be. Naked, touching, rubbing against each other, two tinders striking sparks from the world around them and within them. Ashiike let his hand drift from her pussy to the cleft of her buttocks, dragging moist fingertips across her ass, pressing against the little ring that puckered between the firm globes of flesh.

She shuddered—his *Ma'ay*, his *fox*. Her body moved like a snake about to shed its skin, ripples of arousal just below the surface finding an echo in his own desires. He let the head of his cock replace his fingers, resting it in her shadows, pressing a little, keeping the fire simmering under her passion but containing it, controlling it until he was ready to let it explode and engulf them both.

"My love, my Ashiike . . ." Her whisper vanished on the breeze as she pushed back against him, her hungry quivers letting him know how she relished his touch.

"You are mine. You will always be mine." Ashiike growled the words, swept by a need for her he could not understand or even name. His fox—his prey—his mate.

"Yes . . ." She fell limply to her knees, bowing her head to the rising moon.

He stared at her, back firm and gleaming softly as her hair fell to either side of her neck. She was a wonder of nature, every bit as magnificent as the orb now peering at them from beyond the horizon. Could any goddess be more beautiful than his Ma'ay?

"I want you, Ashiike."

Ma'ay turned a little, glancing over her shoulder. "Take me any way you wish. Whatever your desires—they are my desires too. Just take me. Fill me. *Fuck me . . .*"

Her words only fueled the fire in his cock and the rising swell of passion in his heart. She was truly a fitting mate for a warrior. There would be no question of what she wanted—or why she wanted it. Her ass waggled invitingly as she leaned forward on all fours.

"What are you waiting for?" The challenge was flung at him from ripe lips that curved into a half-smile. "It is there for the taking, my brave Ashiike."

Ashiike narrowed his eyes. "You dare tell me my job, woman?" He dropped to his knees, forcing her thighs apart to make room for him. "Perhaps you need to learn who is master here . . ."

He lifted his hand and smacked one cheek of her ass, a ringing blow that brought the imprint of his palm to the skin, a brand that marked her as his and took the breath from his lungs for a second or two.

"Oh, oh . . . you *devil* . . ." She tossed her hair to one side, licking those lips, panting and waggling some more. "I find I like being *bad* . . ." Ma'ay's quick glance at him from under her eyelashes was both heated and coy, a mixture he found incredibly stimulating.

"And you like the punishment, I think . . ." Once more he smacked her, a little harder this time, making her rock slightly in her prone position.

"Yes, oh *yessss* . . ." Her thighs were wet, shining now in the moonlight. Her scent filled the air, sage and sex and spice and all Ma'ay.

He reached for her pussy, thrusting two fingers through the slick honey and slapping her once more as he did so.

"*Aaiyeeee* . . ." She howled, a sound of pleasure and pain and hunger. "I need . . . I want . . ."

"What?" He lifted his palm and again brought the blood to her ass cheeks with swift stinging blows.

"*I need* . . ."

He moved his fingers inside her, stimulating her, grinning as her thighs spread wider in encouragement.

"Make me *come*, by the Gods. *Make me come* . . . *fuck me*, you bastard . . ." Her head dipped low as she reached for her breasts and Ashiike knew she would be kneading them now, pinching and pulling on the nipples in that particular way that suited her in these moments.

He pushed at her, parting her thighs as wide as he could, making room for himself as he poised the head of his cock between her buttocks. It was awkward for a moment or two, keeping one hand in her cunt and getting himself where he needed to be. But he did it.

Then he pushed inward.

She cried out as he penetrated past the tight muscles into her secret places, but relaxed as he entered slowly, his way greased by his own liquids as they mingled with her juices.

She was tight, very tight, the grasp of her ass around his cock an embrace he would never forget.

It was time. Time to move his hand—just like *that* . . .

She shattered on a scream that filled his world, erupting around him, on him, driving him deep with her spasms and squeezing his cock so tight he thought he might be bound to her like this for eternity.

His balls clenched taut as he thrust, fighting to control the onrush of his own climax.

"Ma'ay . . ."

He roared her name . . .

And woke up.

THREE

*M*IDGE GAVE THE WHOLE construction a tentative tug and was very pleased to see that her tent remained upright and taut. She'd actually managed a respectable assembly and only had to check the directions twice.

The sun had set but there was still just about enough light to ensure that the pegs were well seated and all the various poles snugly married to the appropriate loops. She'd stretched the rain shield over the top, but doubted it would be necessary. There might be showers in the mountains looming nearby, but there was little likelihood that any would make it this far down into the wide valley.

Tolikani Canyon really wasn't a typical canyon, it was more of a flat plain, rimmed with foothills and containing the occasional rifts that in a glacier would have been termed crevasses. It was in one of these that the Anasazi had built some structures and it was near this one that Midge had pitched her tent.

Checking carefully for wildlife, she'd thumped and banged and clattered her way through the process, hoping she'd also scared off any critters that might have been curious about her.

It was an established campsite though, so there was little in the way of shrubbery to conceal any slithery inhabitants. Midge preferred not to use the word "snake." Saying it might attract one. She soooo didn't like snakes.

Satisfied that her little dwelling was secure, Midge stretched and looked skyward. Above her the stars were beginning to twinkle through the darkening heavens and the dying shades of sunset glimmered ever fainter on the horizon.

Even though she was less than a hundred yards from civilization— as represented by the small residence established for the convenience of Tolikani visitors—Midge was out of sight of the low building and for all intents and purposes alone with the desert night.

She breathed in, scenting the sharp tang of the air, unsullied by fumes or other modern scents. It was clean, almost abrasive as she exhaled, cooling rapidly now that the sun was gone.

She was happy in a quietly euphoric kind of way—as if she'd come home to a place that healed her soul. Tiredly, she crawled into her tent and slid out of her shirt and pants, deciding to sleep in her practical cotton underwear rather than struggle with pajamas in her tight quarters.

Resting her head, she closed her eyes.

Only to find nothing happened.

She was exhausted, but sleep was a long way away. She also felt grubby, even though she'd swirled some lukewarm soapy water over her face and hands in the tiny bathroom at the hostel.

The distant rumble of thunder snagged her attention and she got out of her little quilted nest and peered from the tent to see the flicker of lightning high up on the mountain. It was surreal— like a light show on another planet.

Midge watched for a few minutes then tilted her head as she heard the gentle ripple of water. Putting two and two together, she figured that the rain *was* coming down the mountain even though the storm wasn't.

Not far from the tent was a series of ledges and boulders, smoothed by time and—Midge now realized—water. The savvy travelers who had first camped here had done so with a reason.

There was a lovely built-in shower system, complete with pool, mere steps away. And what could be more tempting to a weary and grubby archaeologist than a moonlight shower in the isolation of the desert?

Ooooh. Yeah.

Midge grabbed her shower gel, figured it could double for a shampoo and tucked a towel under her arm as she slipped her feet into that essential traveler's accessory—flip-flops.

Within moments she was standing looking at something out of an impressionist painting. Water cascaded in silvery sheets from the highest ledge to crash into a shallow basin and trickle down over several more large flat boulders to a pool at the bottom of the little hill. The mountains were a shadowy backdrop, silhouetted against an inky sky now brilliant with stars.

She stepped nearer, getting her bearings, checking for solid footings or loose gravel and broken rocks. The moon was rising, full and brilliant and giving her more than enough light to see what she needed to see—a shower, created by nature, ready made for weary travelers to refresh themselves.

Exactly what Midge intended to do. She glanced around, making sure that all was quiet. There was a glow from behind the small ridge where the others were tucked up in the hostel. But for the rest of her surroundings—well, there was pretty much a whole lot of nothing. The absolute darkness of nothing. No streetlights, no houses, no distant towns—it was a blackness that people in the past knew well and people of today seldom experienced.

A blackness that helped Midge understand why so many early cultures had feared the night. It wasn't just the loss of the sun, it was the total lack of any other kind of illumination. At least she had a full moon. What must it be like where there was no softly glowing disk in the sky? When clouds scudded over the stars? It would be a heavy darkness that could easily give rise to legends of terror and fear. A blindness that only the flames of a fire could drive back—and even then, the shadows would lurk at the edges of the camp.

Midge shook off the introspective mood and daringly stripped. This wasn't like her, modest type that she was, but somehow in this place—these surroundings—the trappings of civilization were unnecessary.

Grabbing her plastic bottle and tugging the elastic band from her hair, Midge stepped cautiously under the makeshift shower.

And sighed with delight. The water was *warm*.

How and why she didn't actually care. It was simply an unbelievable pleasure to stand naked in the desert and allow nature to provide the spa facilities.

Cascades of runoff poured down onto her head and shoulders and for a few moments Midge just let it, savoring the gentle massage provided by the pounding stream. Then she reached for her soap and poured out a good amount, lathering herself enthusiastically and loving the whole sensual experience.

The stone upon which she stood still held the remnants of the day's warmth, kind of like standing on heated tiles. It was sybaritic, decidedly decadent, enormously pleasurable and the highlight of Midge's month. Probably, she thought to herself as she scrubbed her belly, the highlight of her year.

It certainly made the long bus trip worthwhile.

Of course, to be very honest, Web Jones had done that.

The time they'd spent together on the bus, their conversation— oh yeah. He'd made her millennium.

So it had been a bit embarrassing to wake from a rather erotic dream of him and find him staring at her.

But she'd gotten to return the favor when he'd dozed off, only to mumble some obscure Anasazi word and grab his crotch.

God forgive her, she'd giggled. But he did have one extraordinarily fine bulge beneath those nice hands. It must have been as erotic a dream as hers had been. The expression in his eyes—the heat—the lust—

An image of his face flickered up into her mind at the precise moment her hands slid below her belly to her crotch and her pussy lips, the combined assault on her senses sending an instant shot of arousal through her body. Her buttocks tightened, her breasts suddenly felt every drip of water that trickled over their nipples and her heart began to thud with a rhythm attuned to the needs of her cunt.

She froze, water still running over her body, sluicing the lather from her skin and hair. Her hands remained between her legs as she explored the new feelings within her. Midge was no stranger to the art of self-satisfaction. Masturbation most often occurred in the privacy of her own bedroom—a matter kept between her and her pink vibrator.

She didn't have one of those pulsating showerheads and most mornings had neither the time nor the urge to bring herself to climax before a long day at the college. So being naked in the wilderness, under a natural showerhead with her hands at her pussy, was—for Midge—*unusual*. To say the least.

It was also amazingly, *incredibly* erotic.

Midge relaxed into the moment, opening herself for once to the possibilities of her body and her own touch. She widened her stance on the rock, settling herself comfortably beneath the water, leaning back so that the brunt of the stream fell across her nipples.

Stimulating and exciting, she moved her hips—a slow swivel accompanied by the caress of her fingers against her clit. The fanciful notion came to her that she was dancing . . . a sensual tango of water-driven desire . . . a ballet of body and hands and sex . . .

The thundering of her blood in her ears provided the drumbeat for her movements and the soft rippling of the waters sang a melody only nature could transcribe. She felt at one with her surroundings—as if the act of pleasure was simply a part of this land, this place, this time.

The moon had shifted slightly, its rays now catching the spray from the water and turning the droplets to rainbows and silver—a fairy-like display of incredible beauty that enhanced the night sky and kissed Midge's skin with magic.

Her hands found places that yearned, her fingers fulfilled that yearning. Sliding one hand to her breasts, she cupped them each in turn, squeezing and kneading the globes, toying with the hard peaks, squeezing until the pleasure was barely a breath away from pain. She was woman—feminine, curved, slick with water and the soft velvet of her own skin.

She was acting out the fundamental principle of life. Doing something that had been done for untold generations by uncounted numbers of her ancestors. She was at one with the night and with the essence of life, slowly bringing herself to an orgasm that would echo so many orgasms before—probably some in this very spot under a similar stream of warm liquid.

The gods of the mountains had shed tears of desire, letting them meander down steep slopes so that she could take them into her body and—*come.*

Perhaps they were watching. Midge closed her eyes and tipped her head back, arching her spine and thrusting her breasts and hips forward into the water. Let them watch. Let the gods enjoy what she herself was enjoying.

She played with her body, teasing herself to a peak then pausing, waiting endless agonizing moments before returning to repeat the process. It increased her arousal, drove all thoughts from her mind and turned her focus inward and down to that small spot that now swelled from beneath its hood.

"Oh dear *God . . .*" She sighed out the words almost without volition as a particularly strong shudder rocked her from toes to eyebrows. She was close—so close—she could almost taste her orgasm in the back of her throat.

She wasn't the only one.

SLEEP WAS IMPOSSIBLE. HE'D tried thinking about his novel. Nothing. Not a teeny iota of inspiration.

He'd tried letting his mind float and his body relax, the way all the books said was guaranteed to induce sleep. Again—nothing.

Web had thumped his pillow, tossed and turned on his uncomfortably tiny cot and cursed himself luridly for not having the forethought to bring a tent.

She had. Miss *There's-something-about-her-that's-getting-to-me* Midge had brought a tent for herself. She was probably tucked up in a sleeping bag inside it right now. Or perhaps she wasn't. Maybe she was lonely. Maybe she was scared . . . like if she'd heard a coyote or something.

Did they have coyotes out here? Duh, of course they did. They ate . . . um . . . those things that popped their heads up out of the ground.

Aaaargh.

Web cursed once more and gave up trying to sleep. Shawna, their driver and the few visitors from other archaeological digs had merged into one beer-guzzling, giggling group which held no attraction for Web at all, Shawna's best seductive efforts notwithstanding.

She'd brushed her breasts against him, flashed him her thong twice and made it quite clear she'd fuck him at the drop of a pickax.

Unfortunately, Web wasn't sure exactly where in the *line to fuck Shawna* that offer put him—before the bus driver? Maybe after the driver and before the other dig-leader? He hoped it was at least ahead of the graduate students. Wherever it was, he knew for sure he didn't want to be there.

He did, when he allowed himself to admit the truth, know *exactly* where he wanted to be and *who* he would've liked very much to be invited to fuck. And she wasn't in the hostel at all, but in a largish pup tent that would hold two at a squeeze.

They could squeeze. He'd like to squeeze.

He'd like to squeeze her full breasts and have her thighs squeeze him as he slipped between them to find her pussy with his cock and plunder her carefully hidden treasure.

She'd made him horny just by being herself and that was a rarity in Web's book. Having a hot dream while dozing right fucking *next* to her was about the most embarrassing thing he could remember doing in a long time.

Web shook his head. It had been a close call. Two more seconds and he'd have come in his pants, thus totally destroying any hopes he'd ever cherished of coming inside *hers*.

He decided to surrender to the inevitable and go find her. If she told him to get lost, so be it. At least he could look himself in the mirror and say he'd tried.

What he found when he'd crept as silently as he could over the small ridge between the hostel and her campsite—well, it had taken his breath away. He wasn't actually sure he'd gotten it back. He might well be dead and peeking into paradise, because what he was watching pretty clearly defined what he imagined paradise to be. And *then* some.

His Midge was naked in the moonlight.

His Midge was wet, standing in a shimmer of water droplets with foam at her feet like some Renaissance painting of the birth of one of the goddesses or other. Right at this moment he couldn't remember who. Or whom. Or whatever.

All his brain cells could come up with was the same phrase, over and over again—*holy fucking shit!*

His Midge was touching herself, playing herself with the pleasure and skill of a virtuoso on an expensive cello. Her head was tipped backward, throwing the line of her throat and neck into the moonlight. It was a slash of white skin that gleamed silver as she moved and swallowed, a lick of brilliance that steered his gaze farther down to her breasts.

Magnificently female, her full breasts swayed and lifted as she shuddered, nipples hard suckable niblets that made his mouth water just by looking at them. She moved every now and again, sighing loudly as the water pounded those peaks, tremors sending crystalline mists of droplets into the night.

Oh my fucking God, what I wouldn't give to . . .

Web's hands were undoing his shirt even as his brain struggled to process the thought. She was Earthmother, Woman-Goddess, the essential essence of half the life on this planet.

He was the other half and his cock was about to kill him or explode. He didn't want either to happen until he'd done exactly what nature had designed him to do—satisfy his mate.

Buttons popped unnoticed, zips ripped apart, pants were tossed carelessly away and shoes kicked God-knew-where. All Web could *see* was her—all Web could *think of* was her—all he wanted to *do* . . . was *her.*

She hadn't heard him, didn't know he was there and coming closer to her shower. Certainly had no clue he was naked and as hard as he'd been in quite some time. His cock thrust proudly in front of him, pointing the way to heaven and Midge.

The moonlight trembled on the swollen head, turning the little drip of desire to a diamond as he walked, heading down to where the object of his lust still thrust her own hand through her pussy lips and panted in time with her movements.

He could smell her, almost taste her already and his own heart-beat accelerated at the mere thought of sinking into her heat.

Carefully he moved behind her, not wanting to startle her any more than was inevitable. She wasn't expecting a nude man to join her. And yet—wasn't that exactly what she needed?

She moaned and Web slipped through the water behind her, placing his hand over hers as she ground her fingers into her pussy. "Yeah, Midge. Oh God yeah. You are so beautiful."

She jerked as he pressed himself against her back. "Jesus Christ. *Web?*" Her pulse fluttered wildly through her entire body as she froze.

"The same. I'm here. Don't stop. Let's take this ride together, baby." He pushed her hand away and delved into her swollen and soaking folds. "Oh wow, you are so fucking hot. So fucking beautiful and naked and hot . . ."

"I . . . I . . . you . . . we . . . oh God . . ." She gasped, but Web noted she didn't pull away. In fact he felt her ass as she tentatively rubbed against his cock.

"I know." He pulled her hard, forcing her back into his chest. "Lift up a bit." He bent his knees and slid his cock between her thighs, through the wetness and slick heat she was producing. "Ahhh, shit that's good. Almost as good as being inside you." He rubbed his cock against her pussy lips, thrusting his hips in time with the movements of his fingers against her clit. "I want to be inside you, Midge. I want to fuck you so bad I'm dying with it. When I saw you—watched you—"

"You . . . you *watched* me?" Her body trembled, but she didn't sound outraged. It was more a kind of leashed excitement.

"Yes. I watched you. I watched you touch these breasts . . ." He fondled the full weights, sliding his hand from one to the other, loving the heat of them as he let them rest in his palm. "I watched you as you played with your nipples . . . like this . . ."

Web teased and pinched the nubs, judging from Midge's responses how far to go, how much sensual punishment to administer. She sighed and squirmed against him, but still made sure she kept his hand where it was.

She was so responsive to everything he did, every place he touched—he was amazed at how in tune their bodies seemed to be.

"I watched you touch your pussy. You found places that made you shiver. I want to feel those places." He found her hand with his. "Show me, sweetheart. Show me where to touch you. Put my hand where you want it."

"I . . ." She hesitated.

He dipped his head and kissed her shoulder, letting his tongue trail a line of warmth from the top of her arm to the dip where her neck rose whitely beneath her tumbled hair. "Do it for me, Midge. Enjoy me. Use me. Let me be your toy." He nipped her softly then kissed the tiny pain away.

"Okay . . ."

It was a breath, no more, but Web heard it and his body pulsed with excitement. Tentatively her hand covered his and guided his fingers to her pussy. She showed him the places that brought her pleasure and the strokes that aroused her. She pushed him lower when her heat built, eventually parting her pussy lips herself and encouraging him to slip two fingers into her cunt.

His cock was soaked with her hot honey, a blend of desire and mountain rainwater that mixed with his own arousal. He wanted to fuck her, to lose himself inside her for a week or two and then repeat the process *ad infinitum*.

This time it was Web who moaned as her body clutched at him, hungry for his invasion. "I want you. I want to fuck you."

"*Yessss . . .*" She groaned out the word, forcing his fingers deep, thrusting her clit onto his wrist and grinding down.

She was nearing her orgasm and Web wasn't sure what to do about it. He wanted to be the one to bring her to the peak, but he wanted his cock inside her while it happened.

He wrenched their bodies apart and spun her around, her hair flying every which way and scattering droplets of the water, which still pattered down on the rocks around them.

"Fuck me, Midge. I want to be inside you. Be with you. Shit, babe . . . let me in . . ."

She cried out as she lifted her thigh to his hip. "*Yes,* Web. *For God's sake . . . now . . .*"

Web thrust forward, choking back a cry of his own as she enveloped him in slick boiling moisture. He rammed himself into her welcoming darkness, aware that she was tensing around him and in his arms even as he entered her.

"*Web.*"

She screamed out his name and his heart swelled within his chest.

Then their world collapsed beneath them and everything went black.

FOUR

"OOOOOWWW . . . *braaaackkk* . . ." Midge coughed and hacked and opened her eyes to see nothing at all. "Fuck. I'm *blind*." Her head ached where she'd whacked it on something, her body was tingling and shuddering and she had the distinct impression that she might have just orgasmed and missed it.

And she'd been enjoying *such* a lovely erotic fantasy about Web too.

"You're not blind. Unless both of us are. It's just pitch-black in here."

Midge froze at the sound of a man's voice. A very *familiar* voice. Holy *shit*. "Hello? Web? Is that you?" She reached out in the darkness only to touch something warm and solid. She jumped.

"Of *course* it's me. Who did you think was fucking you? You screamed my name out very satisfactorily before we fell into . . . wherever we are." He sounded mildly irritated.

She cleared her throat. "Just to get the facts straight here, you *really were* with me under that waterfall? When I was . . . er . . ."

"There was no *er* about it. You were *doing it*. With me."

"And you *were* there? *Really?*"

The sigh was loud and masculine. "Yes. I. Was. There. Okay?"

"Oh dear." Midge wanted the ground to open up and swallow her whole. No wait, it just did that. Perhaps it would obligingly do it again. She buried her face in her hands and groaned. "Oh *deeeeear.*"

There was another sigh, this time a rather exasperated one. "I'm thinking that this is not the time for an attack of maidenly modesty." Noises and scrabblings near where she knelt told Midge that he was standing up. "Ouch."

"What?"

"Low ceiling." He paused. "I just whacked my head on a lump of rock, which shouldn't be there. We fell *down*, right? Therefore *up* should be the way back to the waterfall."

Midge nodded in the darkness, then realized he couldn't see her. "Yes. And, now that you come to mention it, there isn't any water here. It should be wet. There definitely should be puddles or streams or something . . ." She tentatively put her hand around her, feeling sand, gravel and—"*Aaargh.*" Something moved beneath her fingers.

"Let go of my foot."

"Sorry." Midge struggled from her knees to a sort of standing position, staggered and instinctively reached out to regain her balance, grabbing the first thing that came to hand.

Web muffled an odd squawk. "You can let go of *that* too. If we get out of this, I might need it later."

Thankful he couldn't see her blushing, Midge removed her hand from his cock. "Sorry again."

"Don't be." A low chuckle had followed her words. "I like your hand on me. I want other parts of you on me. I want to disappear into that tiny tent with you and not come out for about a week or two."

Midge's jaw dropped. "You *do*?"

"Duh. Yeah. I do indeed." His voice came from a slightly different direction as he explored their location. "I thought you'd have figured that out by now, you being so smart and all and me begging you to let me fuck you . . ."

"Don't be sarcastic. I thought you were a dream." Midge gently moved away from him to find her outstretched hands touching hard rock. This time it was cold and non-human. She breathed a sigh of relief.

"Dream about me a lot, do you?" His tone was amused and seasoned with a dash of totally male satisfaction.

"No." She clamped her jaws shut with a force that made her teeth clash and her ears ring. "Only when I run out of batteries for my vibrator."

"Tsk tsk, Professor. That's a whopping great fib."

Midge let her hands trace a path to the right, carefully checking the sandy floor beneath her feet as she closed her eyes and allowed her other senses to map the room or cavern or whatever it was they'd dropped into. "Web. Shut *up* for a bit, will you? I'm trying to concentrate here."

There was a small snort and then silence, broken only by the sound of two people stumbling around in complete blackness. Inevitably, given a tiny enclosed space, their perimeter investigations brought them to the same place.

"Uhh . . " Midge jumped and gasped as strong hands brushed against her breasts.

"Mmm." The hands turned, squeezed, stroked and fondled affectionately.

"Web?"

"Mmm?"

"What the hell do you think you're doing?"

"Taking advantage of your confusion and disorientation to cop a quick feel?"

"I'm not confused or disoriented. Stop *copping*."

There was a large sigh and the hands reluctantly left her breasts. "You're no fun."

"*Fun?*" It was a screech, but at this point Midge didn't care. "You want *fun?* I'm perfectly capable of having fun. But I have to say that since we're someplace we shouldn't be with no apparent way out, the idea of *fun* isn't at the top of my list of things to do right now."

"Pity."

"Grrrrrr."

There was a chuckle. "Okay. Sorry. Bad timing. Let's see if we can find some way out of this damn hole. We know the walls are solid. Perhaps there's a crack at the top or something. I mean we got in here *somehow* . . . we should be able to get out the same way." He was quiet for a moment. "Do you feel any air? Any draft?"

Midge froze. "You worried about us running out?"

His silence was answer enough.

Midge redoubled her efforts, letting her fingers dapple lightly over every single nook and cranny she could reach. She was absolutely not going to think about the fact that their supply of breathable oxygen might be running out.

She was not going to even consider the possibility that perhaps the two of them were well and truly trapped and their bones would dry out to mummified skeletons before they were ever found.

Of course if they *were* trapped, then she promised herself she was going to use the last of her air up while fucking what was left of the brains of Web Jones out his eyeballs. They would expire joined together. And wouldn't that amuse the hell out of whoever discovered their bodies?

DNA testing would probably . . .

"Hey."

Web's voice pulled Midge from her nightmarishly arousing fantasy. "What you got?"

"I'm not sure, but it feels like carvings of some sort. I need the expert here."

Heart pounding with excitement, Midge stepped toward the sound of his voice. This was one area where she knew she could deliver the goods. She might want Web's body in the worst way imaginable, but that was a fantasy.

Getting them out alive—*that* was reality. Everything else could wait.

HE COULD ALMOST HEAR the throb of the blood through her veins as she neared him. Web had no clue why this particular woman aroused him so, but she did. Fact. It happened—he intended to deal with it. Right now, they needed to get out of this damned hole so that he could get into—well, okay, to be blunt about it—*another* hole.

His cock was still aching, richly flooded with the memory of her silk-wet velvety clasp around his aroused length. He hadn't come before they'd fallen into wherever it was they were and like any normal functioning male, his head wouldn't quite snap into gear until he'd relieved his *other* head.

He sighed and bit down on a pang of lust as her body heat seared his arm. She stopped just short of touching him, which was probably a good thing since he might well have exploded at any more tactile exposure to that soft skin of hers. He'd punished himself with his caresses, needing to know she was there, wanting to explore all of her body and seriously lusting for her to be squirming beneath him as he plundered her.

"Where?"

Anywhere you want baby. "Huh?"

"The carvings? Where are they?" A hand brushed his shoulder.

"Oh those. Here." He slid his arm through the darkness and found hers, folding their fingers together. He raised them both to the place on the wall where he'd found the odd indentations. "Feel them?"

He could hear strands of hair brushing her shoulders as she nodded, a whisper of movement loud in the silence around them.

"All right then." Gently he eased his fingers from her hand, regretfully pulling away.

There was no noise at all for a moment or two other than their breathing. *Hers* a soft intake of breath as she blindly allowed her fingertips to "read" the carvings. *His* a more muted rasp, redolent with heat and need and lust for the woman so close to him—and so fucking *naked*.

He swallowed. "What do you think?"

"Sssh."

"Sorry."

Perhaps he could take her as she stood there, just slip up behind her as he'd done under the waterfall. Perhaps he could tuck his cock between her ass cheeks and explore her little anal muscles for a bit . . . play around with her, arouse her until she was soaking wet and willing to take him any way she could get him.

His cock jerked painfully, balls hard and taut as the images flooded his brain.

"Aha."

He damn near jumped out of his skin. "*What?*"

"Got something. I think." She shuffled her feet a little. "Come here. I want you to feel this and see if you agree."

Obediently, Web stepped to where her voice was coming from.

"Now stand close behind me and put your hands over mine. Then we'll reach upward. I want you to feel one particular set of carvings . . ."

I am going to die. Right this minute, I am going to expire from unfulfilled orgasmic pressure.

Her back tucked neatly into his front as he pressed himself against her. His cock quickly snuggled into the cleft of her buttocks.

She cleared her throat.

Web shrugged. "You're naked. I'm naked. You turn me on. Deal with it." He thrust a little with his hips for emphasis, knowing he was brushing sensitive skin. For additional emphasis he dropped a light kiss on her shoulder.

Midge moaned softly. "*Shitshitshitshit.*" Her ass swayed sensually, encouraging him, massaging him—it would only take a second to—

"Web. For God's sake . . ." She choked out the words. *"Please. One of us has to concentrate here . . ."*

He didn't sob although he was closer than he'd ever believed he could be. "Okay. But I reserve the right to continue this . . ." he thrust once more, *"discussion* at a later time."

"I second that motion." She groaned out the words. *"God."*

"So what am I supposed to be feeling along with the creamy silk of your body . . ."

"Oh *Web.* Creamy silk?" She almost turned, her ass caressing his cock and making him bite back a shriek of need. "Ahem." Midge cleared her throat. "This. Here."

Carefully she guided Web's hands to the wall in front of her, incidentally pulling him absolutely snug against her spine. There wasn't room for a mote of dust to slide between them.

Grinning painfully, Web let his weight lean forward, sandwiching her between him and the wall. Or—as he rather whimsically found himself phrasing it—between a rock and a hard-on.

"There. Do you feel it?"

He had to really focus for a moment or two to remember what she was talking about. Then, beneath his fingertips, he felt more shapes, indentations, man-made depressions in the rock wall.

In spite of his lust, he was fascinated and he relaxed for a second or two, just touching the carvings that had been incised so very long ago. "I feel . . . I feel a squiggle? No wait . . . several squiggles . . ."

She nodded, almost taking out his lower jaw in her excitement. "Yeah. Like hieroglyphics. I think they're Navajo or possibly Anasazi."

"Cool." Web continued to explore. "I feel several squiggles and then above them a V-shape. Inverted. Sort of like a mountain maybe . . ."

"I think you may be right. The squiggles could be water. Water from the mountains."

Web's fingers moved higher than Midge's could reach. "There's more up here. More indentations. Small ones. Four of them. And a large circle."

"Damn . . . I can't . . ."

"Wait a second." Web bent down and put his hands around her hips then straightened, lifting her off her feet.

"Oh better. Thanks."

Now her ass was pressed into his chest and he could lick the base of her spine with just a tiny bend of his head . . .

"Did you just *lick* me?"

"Nope. Not me." Web shook his head as he lied through his teeth.

There was silence for a few more moments then she breathed quickly. "Okay. I think I have it. You can put me down."

Web, lost in the scent of her skin and her pussy, barely heard her.

"Web. You can put me down."

"What?"

"Put. Me. *Down.*"

"Oh. Yeah. Sorry." He lowered Midge back to the floor.

"Right." She sounded a little shaky around the edges of her

voice. "As near as I can figure it, this chamber opens when some-body stands on that rock we were on. Actually, it takes two peo-ple, hence the four little depressions you felt, which represent feet. And, of course, there has to be water falling from the moun-tains. Quite a unique set of circumstances." She sounded rather pleased with her interpretation. "We could be in a sort of *kiva*, a ceremonial chamber . . ."

"That's nice. How do we get out?"

"Well, that's not quite so clear . . ." Midge paused. "But I think it will re-open when the waterfall diminishes. There was a circle with only one squiggle and the circle was open. Does that make sense to you?"

He sighed. It sounded a great deal more like wishful thinking than hard science. But there was a note of desperation in Midge's words. What else could he do?

"Yeah. It makes sense." He stepped back a little. "So all we have to do is wait until the waterfall drops down to a trickle and then something will slide back and let us out?"

"I *think* so." She gulped, a rough noise that told Web how uncertain she was. "Are there any more glyphs higher up?"

Web leaned in once more, just enjoying the feel of her as he reached for the wall. "Nope. That round open one is the top one."

"Good." She sighed, her body rising and falling with her breath. "So all we have to do is wait."

"Okay." Web blinked at the darkness. He wished he could see her. But lacking sight, he had to rely on his other senses. One of which was touch.

He reached out and let his hands find her shoulders, tracing her arms down to her elbows and then her wrists, turning her so that as near as he could tell she was facing him.

"Now . . . while we're waiting, there's something I'd like to discuss . . ."

He pulled her hands into his and rested them against his belly, sliding them down so that her fingers ended up around his cock.

He smiled as they curved naturally into place. "I think we should explore—some more of our surroundings. Don't you?"

FIVE

"T . . . ER . . . " She was holding Web Jones's fabulous cock in her *hand*. Any logical, rational thoughts had just taken a walk down some side street or other and gone into a bar for a beer.

She was left with a head full of the most decadently divine images inspired by the feel of that superb length resting in her palm. Without the benefit of light, Midge had to rely on touch, sensing the shape and dimensions of him through her fingertips just as she had "read" the carvings on the wall behind them.

This time though, there was little—if any—effort required to translate what she was feeling. *De-luscious!* He was heavy and solid, skin surprisingly delicate and fragile beneath her touch. It slid delightfully over the steel of his muscle, delineating the veins and ridges that individualized his cock.

Midge wondered for a moment if they were all unique—if a man's cock was his masculine fingerprint, as different from the next one as his DNA or his retinal patterns. She closed her eyes and breathed in, letting the fragrance of his body add to the picture her mind was creating.

Sweet and male, his scent soared up into her brain and filled out some of the blank spots on her mental painting. She saw once more the curve of his lips as he smiled at something or other and recalled the way his eyes lit up with humor and—possibly—desire.

She ached to see his face, to see what he would look like as she held him. Was he closing his eyes? Was he looking down, vainly hoping to see her hand wrapped around him?

Experimentally, Midge moved, letting her fingers stroke the length of his cock, finding the ridged head swollen and hot to her touch. She sensed the ripple that coursed through Web's body and definitely heard him suck in air as she let her fingers reverse their move, sliding down to the coarse curly hair.

Curiously she delved beneath, finding the soft sac with its precious cargo, taut and high, a miracle of nature in and of itself. His pulse thudded through his balls as she fondled them delicately, his tongue sliding noisily over his lips close to her ear.

"You have wonderful hands, Midge." He whispered the words, breath hot and brushing over her skin like the sensual caress of feathers and fur.

"Thank you." She tightened her grip then released it a little, trying to sense what effect her movements were having on him. It was strange—this blind passion. Almost like being in a dream, yet having something real and responsive to touch.

The darkness was a hindrance and yet in many ways it was a help. It hid her, sheltered her from his gaze, made her almost anonymous—it freed her to explore options that otherwise might not have occurred to her.

"If you don't mind . . ." Hesitantly, Midge lowered herself down to the ground in front of Web. "I'd like to try something here."

There was a strangled groan. "Honey, whatever you want to do, *do*. I'll like anything and everything."

She caressed his cock once more, dropping a kiss on the very tip and finding a tiny slick of moisture there. She tasted it, licking it from her lips. "Mmm. Salty. Man."

He settled into his stance and Midge could tell he had parted his legs wider, allowing her access to whatever she wanted, to do whatever she chose to do.

Rising up on her knees and shuffling forward a little bit, Midge let her breasts rest around his cock, tucking it into the deep cleavage created by the swells of flesh.

He moaned. A definite, *I'm-so-enjoying-this* kind of moan.

"Does that feel good, Web? Do you like that?"

"*Hrmplfmpf.*"

She giggled past her own arousal. "I'll take that as a yes."

It was all the things she'd known a perfect cock would be. Steel and silk, heat and hardness, perfectly shaped to fill the valley between her breasts. And when she began to move up and down, tugging on that delicate skin, his gasp of pleasure was unmistakable. "*Sheeeit*, Midge . . ."

"Let go, Web. I want to make you *let go*." Where all this was coming from, Midge hadn't a clue. She'd never told a man to come in her life, never dreamed she'd have enough nerve to wrap her breasts around his cock—certainly would never *ever* have imagined it would be Web Jones attached to the other end.

Somehow the darkness had stripped away the civilized façade of Dr. Marjorie Hayworth and revealed Midge-the-sensual-slut who was having a wonderful old time for herself as she stroked Web's cock and turned herself on simultaneously.

His breaths grew sharper and faster as she kept the rhythmic movements going, finding additional sharp pleasure from her own hands as she pushed her breasts together, squeezing hard nipples to further enhance the whole experience.

"Midge . . ." He whispered her name, sending shivers of delight through her body. "Jesus, Midge . . ."

His muscles tensed—she could sense them, almost hear them clench around her as she worked him.

Her own body was wet, the sensation of skin against skin erotically arousing, a pleasure not to be denied. Her pussy throbbed and ached and yearned, but this was something she wanted to do for and to Web. It was her moment in the sunshine, metaphorically speaking, although it was pitch-black.

There was some kind of synergistic symmetry to the light and dark thing, but with Web's cock trembling between her breasts, Midge gave up trying to grasp the symbolism and just focused on the sex.

The air around them was rich with the sounds of their bodies as they slid together in a smooth glide of heat and desire. Panting breaths mingled with the soft whisper of skin and the thunderous pounding of Midge's heartbeat.

He gasped, a choking sound deep in his throat and Midge felt his cock shudder. She forced her breasts tightly around it and slid down just as he erupted, jets of hot come dappling her neck and chin.

Tears stung her eyes as he groaned out her name, a sound of satisfaction and delight that came from his guts. She'd done it—she'd pleasured him past his point of control and brought him to his trembling peak.

She, Midge Hayworth, was Woman-Goddess. Her tits were weapons of mass-satisfaction. She had reduced the mighty Web Jones to a heap of shaking stickiness that was now slithering to the floor in front of her, by the sounds of things.

Raising a finger to her skin and touching the droplets of his come, she grinned. "You okay?"

"You're kidding, right?" He sighed and stretched, a hard thigh brushing her legs then snuggling close, staying there contentedly. "I've never been so okay. This redefines everything I ever associated with *okay.*"

Relaxing, Midge sighed too. "Good."

"And if I'm not mistaken . . ." There was a pause.

"What?"

"Well, either the sex was so good I died when I came and the Pearly Gates are right above me, *or* . . ."

"Or what?"

"Look up, honey."

Midge looked up—and saw stars.

THE TWO MEN STOOD side by side in the early dawn, that magic time when it was neither day nor night and yet the promise of light hovered just below the horizon, sending birds flying from their nests to herald the coming sunrise.

"Nice job, Ashiike."

They were alike in build, solid, male—in an earlier lifetime they might both have been warriors conquering the land they surveyed. One of them had been. An observer would have taken them for peers. The observer would never have guessed that one was probably a thousand years older than the other.

"Thanks, Uncle Eddie." The taller man turned and glanced down at the slightly shorter man by his side. "Think we could drop the *boy* thing soon?"

A chuckle answered Web's question. "Sorry. Force of habit."

Web put his arm around his uncle's shoulders. "You're forgiven. Thanks to your tip I've got my woman. My mate. You can call me Fancy Pants Fanny if you want—right now I couldn't give a shit."

"Feels good doesn't it?" Eddie laughed softly. "I remember."

"How is Aunt Jane?"

"Just fine. You should come by and visit sometime. Bring Ma'ay."

"Midge. My foxy Midge. Yeah. Maybe we'll do that."

Web had always cherished a warm spot in his heart for his strange "uncle". A man who had visited his childhood dreams with magical and wondrous stories, who had calmed his fears, helped him through chicken pox when he was so delirious he could have cheerfully raked his own skin off and who had introduced him gently to the legends and truths of the Anazasi.

And Web had realized with time that Edvarde Przybyl *was* Anasazi. His mysterious high-level government job and now his new wife notwithstanding, Eddie was a unique being that shouldn't exist. But he did and Web was glad of it. He was equally glad that Eddie had "adopted" him at an early age. He didn't care why, simply accepting, appreciating and coming to love this odd man with his wondrous skills.

Web didn't question Eddie's powers. To him they were just

part and parcel of his uncle's personality. He could drop in and out of people's heads like it was nothing special. He could take Web places in dreams that no longer existed and hadn't for a thousand years.

He wasn't a frequent resident of Web's brain, but a welcome one. And when they finally met in person just as Web was graduating kindergarten, the bond of friendship was sealed. It had led Web down the path to his novel and—ultimately—to the right woman. Midge.

Who was snuffling quietly in the tent behind them as they whispered to each other. "You can't stay long enough to meet her, I'm guessing."

Eddie grinned. "Actually, I'm not here at all."

"Ah. Okay."

"I just wanted to make sure all had gone according to plan."

Web swallowed. "Pretty much, yeah. I can't lie and say I didn't get a real scare when that damn rock moved and we fell. If I hadn't known that there was an escape, I would've been really pretty fucking terrified. As it was, I *so* wanted to tell Midge it would be okay."

Eddie nodded. "I know. But I'm betting you found . . . er . . . *other* ways to soothe her. And she read the carvings, yes?"

"Yep."

"Good." Eddie glanced at the horizon. "Nearly daybreak. I gotta scoot or Jane will wake up, know I'm traveling someplace and get pissed she wasn't invited to come along."

"Give her my love, will you? I'm really gonna try and get out to see you both soon. Maybe over the semester break . . ."

Web got a firm clap on the shoulder from a surprisingly strong arm. "Do that. Any time."

And Eddie was gone, leaving Web alone in Tolikani Canyon as the sun stretched, yawned and considered the possibility of lighting another day for its family of tiny orbiting planets.

A small sound from the tent behind him attracted Web's attention and he turned from the dawn to hurry back to where his woman lay tangled in a sleeping bag, snoring quietly.

Only now she wasn't snoring. "Web?" There was a little anxiety in her voice. Not much, but enough. The sound of a woman as yet unsure of her new lover.

"I'm here." He unzipped the entrance, folded his long legs like a pretzel and maneuvered himself inside, zipping the door back up as he settled. "Just communing with the dawn."

"Had to pee, huh?"

"I love your practical mind." He stretched out next to her and let his cool skin caress her warm body. "Mmm. You're toasty snuggly."

She giggled and curled up next to him, sliding a thigh over his hip, pulling him tight against her heat and rubbing her pussy right where it would do the most good. "I had a really strange dream."

"You did?" Web's cock was finding the stimulation quite delightful and responding accordingly. It was making it somewhat hard to focus on what she was saying. But he tried. "Did it have something to do with us stuck in an ancient chamber?"

"Nope. Been there, done that. This was . . ." Midge paused. "This was . . . like . . . um . . ."

Web paused in his sensual caresses of her pussy, letting his hand rest on her hip. "What, babe?"

"This was almost real. As if I was looking at an Anasazi

village. The land looked like Tolikani Canyon, but greener. There was the waterfall, but it was in full spate. A river fell down the mountainside in my dream, not a storm runoff. And I saw . . ."

"What did you see?"

"You're going to laugh at me." She nuzzled his chest, licking his nipple.

"Never. I *never* laugh at dreams."

"Well . . ." Midge took a breath. "I saw the chamber open. Web, it's a marriage chamber. A nuptial *kiva*."

There, it was out. And did Midge feel *stupid*. "Honest, I just knew. There was a couple, there were flowers in baskets—you know, those magnificent Anasazi baskets—and the couple went into the chamber. It closed, the people sort of hung around and ate and drank and then . . ."

"Then what?" Web's voice was encouraging and his fingers made little circles on her hipbone as he listened.

"Then they climbed out the top, like we did, stood there and everybody cheered."

"And they both lived happily ever after?"

"I have no clue. I woke up." She snuffled a giggle. "Stupid, isn't it?"

"Not at all. It's quite possible. When it gets light we'll go check it out. There has to be a way in that isn't dependent upon the water. Perhaps with a flashlight and the chance to examine the *kiva* we'll get a better sense of its purpose. Or at least you will. You're the brains of this outfit . . ."

His hand strayed from her hip to her pussy. "Web . . . I think you've wiped my brain clean. I can't think at all when you touch me . . ."

"It's supposed to be that way."

"It is?"

"Oh yeah." He pulled her beneath him and rose above her, a looming shadow against the soft morning light that barely illuminated their tent.

"I want you again, Midge. My Ma'ay. My fox." His lips found her breast and he began to play once more.

They'd loved twice since coming back to the tent and as far as Midge was concerned it wasn't nearly enough. She had a lot of time to make up—a lot of orgasms to enjoy. And a lot of Web was still left to kiss and nibble and stroke . . .

"Are we okay for protection?"

"Of course." Web reached for what was apparently an inexhaustible supply of condoms tucked into the cargo compartments of his jeans. "I'm always prepared."

"You are?" She stilled a moment.

"Well, I have to say that I brought extra along on this trip. I knew you were coming." He chuckled, a rumble of humor deep in his chest that rebounded off her body. "Or, to rephrase, I *hoped* you'd be coming. With *me*. Like this."

Midge groaned. "Bad pun." She parted her thighs and wriggled her way to the perfect spot beneath him. His cock sank into her slick heat and they both sighed. "Good feeling."

"The best." He leaned his forehead against hers for a moment and she relished the fullness inside her. Web *fit*—his length seemed designed to meet the specifications of her cunt. Just the right dimensions to bring her the maximum pleasure.

How *was* that? How did that happen? Magic? Testosterone? Pheromones? Did it matter?

Web began to move and Midge abandoned her train of thought. It didn't matter how it happened, what mattered was that it *had*. And the odds were pretty good that along with a wonderful lover, Midge had also made an important archaeological discovery. There would be papers and photos and her chairwoman would be delighted.

All things considered, this dig had worked out well for Dr. Marjorie Hayworth. She felt the electricity build inside her as she prepared to enjoy yet another orgasm under the skilled guidance of the sensational Dr. Webster Jones.

Yep. Life in the past was a source of endless fascination, but this particular moment in the present sure was *good*.

"SO WHERE THE HELL were you?" Jane Przybyl raised herself up on her elbow and stared accusingly at her husband.

"Er . . ." Eddie swallowed. "Visiting family?"

Jane raised an eyebrow. "If you had one of your dream trips and didn't take me along, I'm gonna be seriously pissed, you know . . ."

Eddie grinned. "Yeah I know. I told Web that very thing. He sends his love, by the way."

"Ah." Jane didn't look convinced.

"He found his woman. I gave him the teeniest little bit of advice and he's a happy dude now."

"Hmm. Matchmaking?" Jane leaned back on Eddie's arm. "Seems there's no end to your Anasazi talents."

"You should know." Eddie slithered down in the bed and bur-rowed under one of Jane's thighs, emerging between her legs with a wicked smile. "Have I shown you this particular talent lately?"

It wasn't Anasazi, or any particular culture. It was simply a man loving his woman and putting a smile on her face. A fundamen-tally wonderful event that transcended time, history and race.

And still does.

STATUESQUE

LANI AAMES

ONE

THE WEATHERED PEAK OF the rock formation pointed toward the sheer blue cloudless sky. Lia Morgan shaded her eyes against the sun and studied it. She thought it was shaped a little like the prow of a gigantic ship tipped back and half-buried in the desert sand.

"This is it!" Mac shouted and started climbing for a flat table of rock at its base.

Lia watched him. She had been half in love with Mac Taylor since she first met him in college. He had taken her under his wing, shown her how to have a good time, and promised her adventure. Mac had partially filled a void in her protected and pampered life, and Lia was grateful for their friendship even if a little disappointed it hadn't gone further.

Now thirty, he was five years older than she, but he had bummed around a few years before settling on studies in anthropology, specializing in archaeology. He liked the past, he said, better than the present.

In many ways, Lia agreed. The past seemed more interesting and less complicated than the present. Ancient civilizations and antiquities had always interested her, but even so, she hadn't followed that course of study. She had majored in the more practical business and marketing, going for a lucrative career instead of adventure. Yet here she was, spending another vacation following Mac in search of the life-size statue of Zamar and the elusive Zamarians.

If Mac had ever asked her outright, she would have told him she didn't think the statue or the Zamarians existed. All he had was a few paragraphs in a musty old tome written in the latter half of the nineteenth century by a quasi-archaeologist whom everyone else in the field considered a nutcase.

She couldn't blame him for getting his hopes up when he'd discovered a map in yet another batch of scrolls he'd picked up on the black market. Usually the disintegrating sheets of papyrus were nothing more than bills of lading or a merchant's daily tally of goods bought and sold. Interesting because of their age, but nothing unique. Until the map.

How had anything as unusual as the map passed through the hands of a pirate who should be on the lookout for something more valuable? Mac had explained most black marketers were ignorant illiterates looking to make a quick buck. She supposed he was right.

Mac looked back and waved at her to get moving. Lia started climbing over the rocks to reach the flat table. As she laid her hands on each timeworn boulder, they seemed somehow familiar. She shook her head and continued climbing. How many rocks had she and Mac clambered over the past few years? Too many, and they were all starting to look alike.

Whether this led to the cavern Mac sought or not, she hoped this put a rest to his search once and for all.

She reached the flat top and stood, looking at the sand spread out as far as the eye could see. The sun hung low in the western sky to her right, even though it was still early in the evening. Mac had insisted they do this in mid-autumn, on the night the Zamarians held their sacred ritual when the sacrifice of a virgin would bring the statue of the god to life. The midpoint between the autumnal equinox and the winter solstice. The night the boundary between the natural and the supernatural was most easily crossed. It was quite fitting they commence this crazy search on All Hallow's Eve—Halloween night.

The jeep, a few yards from the base, suddenly looked out of place.

"Magnificent view, isn't it?" Mac said.

Lia barely managed a nod. The scene before her wavered as if it were going in and out of focus. She placed a hand on a nearby boulder to steady herself. Dizziness swept over her and she wondered if the desert heat had finally gotten to her. She heard Mac climb down the other side of the flat rock and knew she should follow, but her legs seemed rooted to the spot.

"C'mon, Lia. I found the entrance," he called to her over his shoulder.

She opened her mouth to call out to him for help but couldn't speak. The landscape before her blurred, went black, then . . .

The setting sun burns the desert fiercely with its red and orange golden glow. She lingers on the flat rock waiting for the sand to swallow the fiery orb. She has managed to escape her guards once again, but it becomes more difficult each time.

Although her shoulders are burdened with great guilt, her heart is light because she will soon meet with her lover—the boy who was her playmate in childhood and the man who became a priest because she could never wed.

A lover who is not a lover, she muses as twilight settles across the stretch of sand. She scrambles from the rock, into the hidden entrance . . .

"Lia!" A hand clamped on her shoulder, and she nearly jumped out of her skin. Breathing hard, she whirled to face Mac.

"Are you all right?" he asked, but his dark green eyes were narrowed.

She had first fallen for his eyes. They were almost jewel tone, like emeralds. An unusual combination with his jet-black hair and swarthy skin.

"Yeah," she said breathlessly, as if she had been running. The vision jarred her, but for some strange reason it didn't really frighten her. She sensed a deeper meaning behind it, but a meaning she couldn't quite grasp.

Lia brushed past Mac and leapt from the table of rock. She wound her way through the jumble of boulders, heading straight toward the entrance. She waited for him to catch up.

He looked at her, his head tilted to one side, a strange look of expectation on his face she couldn't explain. "How did you know where to find the entrance? You can't see it from up there. The way it's hidden behind that outcropping of rock, you can't see it until you're right on top of it."

If she told him about the vision, he would think she'd gone mad, wouldn't he? She'd never kept a secret from Mac. But now . . . something deep inside her warned her not to tell.

She shrugged and pointed to the sand. "I followed your footprints."

He looked down and his gaze followed his first set of prints that led to the entrance and back again.

"No shit, Sherlock," he said more to himself than her and laughed.

Mac's sarcasm grated on her nerves. Usually she enjoyed his razor-sharp wit, a little black and a little dry, but suddenly she wanted to lash out at him. Not knowing where the feeling came from, she watched him walk to the opening in the rock face and disappear inside. She followed more slowly.

She stepped inside the tunnel. It was cooler here in the darkness. She swiped at the blonde strands of hair that had escaped her ponytail and fallen across her eyes, plastered to her skin with sweat. She pulled the flashlight from her utility belt and switched it on. The light wavered, in and out, and she wondered if the battery was going dead . . .

She pauses only long enough to light an oil lamp. She has passed this way so many times she could find her way to the appointed place with her eyes closed, but she moves faster with the light to show the way. She runs along the hand-carved passageway, passing entrances to chambers and other tunnels. Most of them lead nowhere, to confuse those not initiated in the ways of the goddess, but her lover has told her how to navigate the maze. She approaches the first fork.

"Where are you going, Lia?"

Mac's call interrupted the vision. Or the vision ended just as he called. Lia wasn't sure.

Lia turned around and flashed her light. Mac had turned right and she had turned left. Had the woman turned left in the vision? In her mind, Lia replayed what she had seen.

Lia remembered the woman running, not bothering to glance to either side. She had almost reached where the main passageway forked, but Mac had called to her, bringing Lia back to the present. So no, the woman hadn't made the turn before the vision ended. Yet Lia had automatically turned left.

"The way to the Chamber of Zamar is marked on the map," Mac said and held out one of several copies he had made because the original was too fragile to survive much handling. "We're supposed to go right at the first fork."

Lia pretended to study the piece of paper. She knew the left passageway would take them where they wanted to go. She didn't know how she knew, but she suspected she was somehow tapping into the knowledge of the woman in the vision. Lia looked at the map in earnest. The left passage led to a few more turns then a dead end . . . according to the map.

She should tell Mac about the visions and how she inhabited the woman, but as soon as she opened her mouth, her vocal chords seemed to freeze up. Her throat muscles seized and she panicked.

"All right!" she screamed in her head. *"I won't say a word!"*

As soon as she made the conscious decision not to tell Mac, her throat relaxed and she was able to breathe again. She took in silent gulps of air, trying to steady her shaking hands.

"Do you see it?" Mac asked sharply and Lia sensed he was losing patience with her.

She swallowed hard. "You're right."

Side by side, they started down the corridor to the right.

"Except?" Mac prompted, flashing his light over the walls and arched ceiling.

Lia smiled. He could hear the doubt in her voice.

"What if the map is misleading? Why would anyone go to the trouble of creating this maze of tunnels and rooms, then leave a map lying around for just anyone to find?"

"But no one found it, Lia. I was just incredibly lucky to run across it in that last batch of scrolls. What are the odds!"

What were the odds? Unbelievably astronomical.

Incredible. Unbelievable. Weren't those words telling her *something*?

"What if it doesn't lead us to the Chamber of Zamar? Or if it does, what if it's a trap? Haven't you seen *Indiana Jones*?"

"That's a movie," Mac snapped. His tone had an edge to it she didn't like. "This is different."

But Lia couldn't leave well enough alone. She was edgy, her senses heightened. She was being pulled in the opposite direction, but had no idea how to get Mac to agree to go the other way without telling him about the visions.

"What if the statue isn't there?" she asked irritably. She truly wasn't trying to provoke him. The chatter helped her to burn off nervous energy. "And even if it is, it has probably been destroyed. Most old tombs and temples were raided of their valuables centuries ago."

"Not this one. There's not a sign anyone has been in here since the beginning."

The beginning of *what*? Did she even want to know? Sometimes, she felt Mac knew more than he was telling her. It was fitting she had her own little secret. If this path did lead nowhere, then they could always turn around and do it her way.

Assuming they survived.

"We have no idea what we're walking into," she continued. "We're crazy for even being here. A team of experts needs to see this. It needs to be recorded and protected."

Mac stopped in his tracks and shone his beam directly into her eyes. The sudden brilliance hurt and she put her hand up, shielding her eyes from it.

"What the fuck am I? Don't you think I know what I'm doing?"

"Get that light out my eyes!" she snapped and gasped in relief, rubbing her eyes when he moved the light away. "You know what I mean, Mac. Of course I think you know what you're doing or I wouldn't be here with you."

"Then why are you going over ground you've covered a dozen times before? We're here now. We're about to make the discovery of the millennium, this one and the last, and all you can do is question me." Mac started down the corridor again. "Just shut the hell up and enjoy it. It's the adventure of a lifetime."

He was right, of course. How many sales reps got the chance to search for a lost civilization that most reputable archaeologists didn't even believe had existed? She should be grateful Mac let her tag along. Maybe, after he'd made his name in the field with this discovery, she could go back to college, get her degree, and join him in his work. He had always resented that he couldn't change her mind about her studies. Then maybe she could change his mind about sleeping with her.

They consulted the map frequently although Mac seemed to have the path memorized. Corridor followed corridor going deeper and deeper. A couple of hours later, they stopped to rest.

Lia watched Mac drink from his canteen, his head tilted back. His long coal-black hair hung limply down his shoulders, tangled

with sweat. She had been half in love with him from the beginning of their friendship, but she knew she could never be completely in love with him. There was a streak of cruelty in him that
kept her from giving her heart to him.

She didn't quite understand why he wouldn't sleep with her.
He said it would ruin their friendship and she knew he was right.
But she was so physically drawn to him that she often grew hot
and wet just watching him do something as simple as taking a
drink. Under normal circumstances, when her clit throbbed and
she ached all over after spending time with Mac, she would lie
in her bed and take care of her needs, pretending it was a black-
haired, green-eyed man who touched her.

To add to her confusion, sometimes it wasn't Mac. Lately, most
of the time it wasn't Mac. His face wouldn't quite come into focus
and all she was aware of was long waves of black hair and emerald
green eyes. Occasionally, she dreamed of him. In her dreams, it
was never Mac, but this other fantasy man.

She couldn't imagine who this other man was. She had never
met anyone else with Mac's black hair, green eyes, and dark com-
plexion. Of course, he didn't really exist, but once in a while she
found herself searching crowds for him. She soon came to realize
the color combo of black hair and green eyes was rare. She further realized that she had invented this man because Mac rejected
her.

Even if Mac agreed to sleep with her, could she actually do it?
She had dated a number of men. She was reasonably attractive
and kept physically fit because of Mac's explorations. Some man
was always asking her out. There had been a few who were warm
and funny and she could almost imagine a life with one of them.

There had been several she had been tempted to sleep with. But when it came down to the nitty gritty, even so far as getting undressed and into bed, she couldn't do it. She froze, her muscles seizing up as stiff and unresponsive as the statue Mac searched for. She always apologized profusely, but it embarrassed her completely. Why was she so different from her circle of acquaintances who talked about sleeping with men as easily as they talked about trying on a new dress?

Most of the men ranted and raved, called her a bitch and a cock-tease as they jerked on their clothes and stormed away. Only two had reacted like gentlemen. With them, she had discovered other ways of pleasure, with lips and tongues and fingertips. One had lasted only that night. He was apologetic, but he didn't have the patience or desire to teach a virgin about sex, to help her get over whatever baggage she was carrying.

The affair with the other had lasted a few months, but every time she tried to make love with him, she would freeze. He never grew frustrated or angry with her. She would more than make up for it by giving him long sessions of blowjobs that left him gasping and shuddering. He would reciprocate, although her body would not allow penetration of her vagina even with his fingers or tongue. They drifted apart, as she knew they would. No man, no matter that he was receiving the best head in his life, could go long without traditional sex.

What was wrong with her? There had been no sexual abuse or molestation in her childhood. She'd had wonderful parents, both gone now, who had been devoted to each other and her. As an only child, she had been spoiled, of course, by their undivided attention, but they had been neither too strict nor too lenient. Her parents had never pushed her to excel although they expected her to do as well as she could. Their unexpected and untimely deaths in a car accident a year after she had graduated from college left her with a little money to invest, which would ensure her a comfortable retirement.

Her parents' unconditional love might be the problem, but she had never equated her parents' love with that of a man. She had always considered herself well-adjusted with no self-esteem problems. She was boringly average in every way. Except she could not have sex.

She shouldn't have let her thoughts stray to her unsatisfactory love life because when Mac suggested they should move on, she could barely stand. She was horny and there was no relief in sight. Fine time for her body to stir and long for a man. She wondered what Mac would do if she jumped him right then, tore the khaki clothes from his body, and rode him like the sex-starved woman that she was. Would he push her away?

More than likely, she thought as she fell into step beside him. He had always been adamant their relationship not pass the boundary of best friends. Lovers, he said, always *cum* and go, but friends, and enemies, lasted for-fucking-ever. Well, that was Mac. Crude but truthful.

Lia let Mac lead the way because if given the opportunity, she would turn around and go back. She didn't trust herself to follow the map. Yet, she didn't trust her instincts. It had been hours since she'd had a vision and she had begun to think they had been her imagination working overtime, carried away with the ambiance of this place.

They had made a few more turns and traveled a few more corridors when Lia, now lagging a few yards behind Mac, nearly lost her footing in the sand. She reached out to the wall to steady herself and . . .

As she nears the chamber, her sandal scuffs against stone, and she stumbles, the lamp falling from her grasp. The oil spills and the light is snuffed out in the layer of loose sand covering the floor. In the sudden darkness, she becomes disoriented and reaches out to steady herself, but she is caught by strong arms and brought up short against a massive chest.

For a moment, she cannot breathe. What if he is not her lover? What if others have discovered their trysts, and now one of them holds her captive? It would mean her death! But more, it would mean the death of her lover.

"Are you sure you're okay?" Mac asked.

Lia blinked. She found herself in Mac's arms, her hands pressed to a chest that bulged to fill his khaki shirt quite nicely. His chest couldn't be called massive, but he had always been muscular and fit.

"I-I'm fine," she assured him and dragged her hands away from him. She was close to tearing the shirt open and pressing her lips to his bare skin. Sexual heat thrummed through every nerve. God, she had never been this aroused! She longed to grab Mac's hand, jam it down her khaki shorts, beneath her panties, and get rid of that awful, sweet ache. As close as she was to the edge of orgasm, it wouldn't take more than a few soft strokes around her clit.

Lia shuddered with the thought and was glad Mac had turned away. She had taken a few steps backward when she realized what she was doing and forced herself to follow Mac.

"Only a few more turns and we're there. These fucking passages are longer than they look on paper."

Lia could only grunt in agreement. She didn't trust her voice. If she tried to speak, she might scream. Every step vibrated through her body. The shorts rubbed between her legs and her panties were damp with her juices. She tugged at them to move them away from her overly sensitive flesh, but after a few steps, they rode up again, tormenting her.

She wanted to strip them off and wallow in the sand until Mac saw her and fucked her as she had longed for him to do ever since she'd met him. She imagined his green eyes dark with passion. No, not Mac's . . . but whose?

Mac had stopped. He shone his light through an opening, but it barely penetrated the darkness.

"This is it," he whispered.

TWO

*L*IA DIDN'T REMEMBER MAKING those last few turns. All she was aware of was her body and the ripples of arousal flowing through her limbs. Her breasts felt swollen and her erect nipples rubbed almost painfully against her shirt; the thin, taut material of her stretch bra only heightening the sensation. She wanted to place her hands on them and massage the ache away, but Mac would think she had lost her mind. Maybe she had.

Shaking her head, trying to clear it enough to concentrate on Mac and his find, she stepped closer to him.

"After you," she breathed.

"No, we do this together," Mac said with a strange smile that she saw in the glow of their flashlights. It didn't look like a smile of triumph but was more of a cat-that-ate-the-canary kind of smile.

Lia shrugged and moved to his side. They stepped inside. Shining their lights around, Lia was shocked to see they were in a natural cavern, not manmade. It was huge, the slope of the ceiling rising away from them into pitch black. Stalagmites and stalactites dotted the ceiling and uneven floor. Rocks, boulders, and mounds of pebbles were strewn everywhere.

There was no sign that any ritual had ever been held here. No statue of the god Zamar.

They stepped away from the opening and the walls groaned around them. She heard shrieking, grinding mechanisms, then walls slamming against walls from near and far. Her eyes grew wide and she started to step back through the opening, but Mac grabbed her arm and pulled her away.

"Look!" He pointed.

The sides of the opening moved together swiftly. She could have been caught between them.

There was a moment of deafening silence when all Lia could do was stare at their only means of leaving this place.

"Oh, Mac, what if we're trapped?" her voice echoed hollowly in the large chamber.

Before Mac could respond, the sounds came again. Some from a far distance and others closer. And one sounded as if it was in the chamber with them. They shone their lights around until the beams caught another exit opening up a dozen yards to the left.

All fell silent again.

Mac laughed. "The corridors changed, and the map is now useless."

"How the hell are we going to get out of here?" Lia asked, her voice surprisingly calm when she wanted to scream in frustration at being trapped. Her body craving a sexual release that was so totally inappropriate it was ludicrous wasn't helping either.

"Through there," Mac said and flashed his beam toward the new opening. "But first we look around."

"There's nothing here!" Lia shouted and her echoes bounced off the walls again and again. "It was a trap. We'll never find our way out if there even is a way out."

"You don't know that, Lia." Mac's voice was calm, reassuring. Too calm. Mac was always sensible in the face of danger, but there should have been some sign of panic as he fought to control it.

She saw nothing but complacency and that frightened her more than the thought of never finding a way out.

"You go that way and I'll go over here," Mac suggested, using the beam to indicate she should go left.

"What are we looking for?" Lia shivered with sexual tension and fear and her voice reflected it, but Mac didn't seem to notice.

"Anything that looks odd. Some sign the Zamarians used this chamber for their ritual. This might well be it, Lia. They made the tunnels that led to this cave to perform their ritual in a natural setting."

It made as much sense as any of this did, she supposed, and did as he told her. She climbed boulders and squeezed between stalagmites, hoping to find some indication that anyone had ever used this cavern for anything. All she saw were rocks and more rocks, as she flashed her light around and the fingers of her free hand pinched at one nipple. When she realized what she was doing, she dropped her hand.

Mac was somewhere on the other side of the cavern. If she had a few minutes she could ease this tortuous ache quickly. She felt her face grow warm in embarrassment. How could that be the foremost thought in her mind when they might die here?

"Find anything?" she shouted.

"Not a thing," he called back and she was disappointed that he sounded too near. It sounded as if he was coming back toward her.

Her only defense was that if she could get rid of her need, she would be able to think more clearly.

She waited a few minutes, but didn't hear his footsteps.

"Mac?" Her voice reverberated softly around her. She waited a few more minutes. "Mac, did you find something?"

There was still no answer. Panicking, she hurried back toward the place where they'd separated.

"Mac!" she screamed. "Can you hear me?"

The floor in this cavern was covered in mottled sand, a mix of black and gray, not the neutral beige color of the desert and layered sand in the passageways. She saw his footsteps trail to a line of boulders he had climbed, but there was no return track. She ran to the boulders and shone her light beyond them. She could see clearly that he wasn't here. He hadn't fallen and struck his head. He wasn't hiding out to tease her.

"Mac, where are you?"

Her echo was the only answer she received.

She made her way to the new exit, but the sand around the opening lay undisturbed. He hadn't gone out without her, but where had he gone?

"MAC! MAC! MAC!" she screamed as long and as loud as she could, until her throat felt raw and her breath was almost gone.

Gasping for air, Lia made her way back to the line of boulders. He might have fallen in a way that she couldn't see. Or dropped into a pit. Or a poisonous snake might have bitten him, paralyzing him, after he stumbled into a far corner. Any number of gruesome things might have happened and she imagined them all as she climbed over the rocks and landed in the sand beyond.

She flashed her light around, but there was no sign of distress. In fact, there were no footprints at all. Mac had never made it this far. She climbed back upon the boulders and looked at them all. They were wedged tightly together, no crevice for him to have fallen through.

Where had he gone?

From where she stood, facing the way they had come in, there was only the cavern wall to her left and a thick column of rock that seemed to be holding up the ceiling to her right. She had been exploring on the other side of the column. He couldn't have gone behind the column or she would have seen him.

She dropped to the ground. She was still shaking, more with fear now, but her breasts and clit still burned where her clothes rubbed them. She had to fight the urge to strip the offending material from her body.

She shook her head to clear it. What should she do? Stay here where she'd last seen Mac in the hopes that he would be able to return from wherever he'd disappeared to? Or go through the new exit and try to find the way out and call for help?

Call! She struggled with her backpack and nearly ripped it open in her anxiety. The radio! It wouldn't reach outside, but maybe she could reach Mac.

She pressed the button. "Mac! Mac, can you hear me?"

She strained to hear beyond the static in case he had somehow gotten far away from her. She called him again and again, but received no answer. At last, she gave up, deciding to save the batteries. If he was unconscious now, he might wake up later and try to contact her.

Deciding to wait here for now, she sat in the dark sand and leaned back against a boulder. She pulled out her canteen, only allowing herself one deep swallow. She hadn't seen any sign of water at all even in this cavern.

All Lia could do now was wait. She rested her head on the boulder and closed her eyes . . .

"My One," a caressing voice whispers in the dark, and she relaxes against him, pressing her palms flat over the expanse of skin between the open folds of his robe. A fingertip on each hand brushes a nipple and they harden beneath her touch. She is pleased by his sharp intake of breath, and the growing proof of his desire pushing toward her.

"I have missed you, Beloved," she murmurs. She is glad there is darkness for it hides the tears she sheds in sadness. "Please, let us leave now. Tonight. I do not know how much longer I can bear to be separated from you."

His lips brush hers, caress her cheeks, and kiss away her tears. She smiles. She should have known that he would be aware of her tears.

"Soon," he says, his voice filled with promise. She clings to it with all her heart. "We cannot abandon our people and leave them at the mercy of the Dark Priest."

She knows he is right, but she senses that if they do not leave soon, they might never leave at all.

"They will not listen. He is the one they follow, that our people have always followed. How can you turn them all against him?"

They dare not say names, that of the Dark Priest or their own, in case someone suspects and listens to them in the dark. Yet, who else would they be speaking of? There is only one priest who wields such power.

"I am not the only one who sees his corruption. Others have joined me in the fight against him. As soon as there are enough, we will defeat him. When that is done, you and I will be free to leave all of this behind."

His hands run over her skin as he speaks and she shivers in anticipation. She slips the robe over his broad shoulders and kisses the hollow at his throat.

"It will not be easy, my One. Your father—"

"My father will not stop us!" *she cries out in defiance although she is fearful he will do just that. They dare not make proper love because if her maidenhead is discovered to be broken, she will die at her father's decree. The virginity of the king's eldest daughter is sacred. Its loss would bring a generation of darkness and war, plague and pestilence to the kingdom—so the followers of the goddess Seniha believe.*

"On your father's command, his soldiers will follow us to the ends of the Earth to avenge Seniha's loss. You know this."

She nods in the darkness, against his chest.

"But we will hide, my One, where no one can ever find us. We will go where they will not know to look. This world is larger than you know, and there are lands across the ocean that will be our refuge."

Lands across the ocean . . . her lover knows so many things of which most others do not.

"Are they arid lands, Beloved?" *she asks in a whisper, her lips teasing his skin. "Or lush mountains and fertile valleys?"*

"Both," *he breathes into her hair as he unfastens the cloth that binds her breasts. "Lush mountains,"* *he says with wicked teasing in his voice as her breasts overflow his large hands.*

She wets her lips and bends her head, placing his thumb in her mouth, suckling in imitation of another part of his body. His breath quickens and he uses her wetness to run lazy circles around the nipple, bringing it to hardness.

His hands skim her ribs and stomach. "Flat plains," he says. He strips away the length of cloth wrapped around her hips, and his fingers tangle in her nether curls. "Grasslands as far as the eye can see." His finger dips and she gasps, her hips surging toward him at his tender touch. "And the most fertile of valleys. You are my world, my life, my love. You are my One forever."

"Forever," she echoes and her heart melts. Her fingers dig into his shoulders, and she throws back her head as he begins to summon that most delicious of feelings from deep inside the center of her being. Her senses heighten and her body arches, as taut as a bowstring.

A wail started low and built with intensity, and Lia was barely aware the sound came from her as she shuddered with the explosion of heat throughout her body, rushing from where her fingers moved round and round her clit and labia, through her limbs, to her toes. Her back rose from the boulder she leaned against as her hips convulsed against her hand. Her other hand had cupped one breast, pinching the hard nipple until pain mixed with the pleasure.

Even in her state of abandon, she didn't dare dip her fingertips into her wet vagina because she knew she would freeze before she could do it. But she craved *something* there. Anything long, hard, and phallic would do, and the thought of a cock, velvet-smooth and deep inside her made her fingers circle her clit furiously, wringing every sensation possible. She roiled with the waves, the sound from her parched throat growing louder and begging for release.

After what seemed an eternity, the last tremor wound down and Lia opened her eyes, wincing at the last echo of her cries. Now she could remember how the chamber had filled with her ragged voice, multiple reverberations sounding like a dozen women screaming in ecstasy.

Lia leaned back against the boulder again and stiffly pulled her hand from her shorts. She was gulping in air and her mouth was as dry as the desert, her tongue like sandpaper. She fumbled with her backpack, legs still spread wide, aching with the aftershock.

She twisted the top off the canteen and poured the cool water down her throat. Even as she drank, she smelled her dew on her hand, and the burn stirred deep inside. Dear God, she couldn't go through that again! She jerked the canteen away from her lips. She wanted to scrub her hand, get rid of the smell, but she couldn't waste the precious water. She'd already drunk more than she should. Half the canteen was gone. Carefully, she closed the top.

The tang of sex had already sent her senses reeling. Her clit and nipples started to throb, a dull rhythm matching the beat of her heart. She had to do something, to get her mind off of it.

"Mac! Mac! Where are you?" she screamed although her voice was hoarse from her earlier shouts and the keening of her tortured release.

There were only his footprints leading to the boulders, none away from them and none on the other side. None leading to the new exit created by the shifting walls. She could wait here, but she could wait until she died of thirst and Mac might still never find his way back from wherever he had gone. That was their only chance, wasn't it? If she could find the way out again and go for help.

Lia threw on her backpack and ran for the exit. Whatever she faced out there was better than waiting here for a slow death. At least out there she would die trying to do something.

Lia stepped across the threshold. She had taken two steps when she heard the shrieking mechanisms start up again. Rock slammed into rock. Gears and chains ground and shuddered. The

opening behind her closed. Then it all began again as new door-
ways were made.

Flashing the light where the opening had once been, she could
barely see the fine line where stone met stone. The precision with
which the blocks were carved and matched seemed impossible
without more sophisticated tools than the ancients had.

But all she had to do was remember Stonehenge, the Sphinx,
and the pyramids of Egypt and South America. The ancients had
more skill and patience with their crude tools than most modern
engineers.

No passages to the left or right. She had no way of knowing
if the maze had returned to its original layout or changed into
another entirely different one. She had no choice. There was only
one way to go, forward.

Lia hurried along the tunnel. She tried to keep her bearings in
relation to the large cavern she'd left behind, but after a few turns
she was thoroughly confused. She stopped to catch her breath
and closed her eyes for a moment. She had been drawn in a different direction since she first entered this place and experienced the
first vision. If she emptied her mind and quit fighting the force,
perhaps it would lead her to where she needed to go.

Making her mind go blank was more difficult than she thought.
She was almost in a state of panic at losing Mac. She pictured
Mac. Tall, handsome, muscled. Long black hair, green eyes . . .
and suddenly he wasn't Mac, but she didn't know who he was.

He was taller, broader, more muscular, but she couldn't glimpse
his face. He was someone she knew intimately, but the practical
part of her reminded her that she knew no one else like Mac. Lia
tried to shake the thoughts away. She needed to concentrate.

It took a while for her to loosen up enough to do it, but for a moment, that breathless time between one second and the next, she managed a perfect state of unawareness. And in that moment, she knew exactly where she needed to go.

Lia ran as fast as she could, turning corners at a reckless pace, sprinting down the straight passageways, until she developed a stitch in her side that forced her to slow down.

Panting from exertion, she reached the end of the first passageway, where she had gone left and Mac right. She shone her light down the long passage. At the end of the tunnel was the way out. She could see if Mac had made it out. If not, she could take the Jeep to the nearest village and bring back help.

Or she could take the left turn. It didn't matter if she set off more traps, she could always find her way back here. She now knew this place like the back of her hand. Whatever connection she had with the woman in the vision gave her the knowledge to find her way no matter the design.

Lia had to discover what pulled at her.

With one last look down the main tunnel, she started at a trot down the left passageway, limping in deference to the pain in her side.

This tunnel looked no different than any of the other dozens she had traveled, but it *felt* different. Moving away from this direction had filled her with doubts and dread. Now, she felt joyous, tingling with anticipation. She felt as if she were going to meet her lover . . . the way the woman had felt in the vision.

With every step she took, her sexual tension grew until she rubbed first one breast and then the other to try to relieve the ache. Even though she was only making it worse, she couldn't stop.

Lia made a few more turns and found herself in a short passageway. Instinctively, she knew this was where the woman had dropped her oil lamp and met her lover in the dark. Here, he had caressed her, murmuring words of love, bringing her to the point of orgasm. Lia whimpered as everything went black. The vision was taking over again.

Her hips undulate in opposition to the swirling of his fingertips, and she longs for him to push inside her wetness. He dares not, but he knows exactly where to touch and what to do and he does it so well. She cannot imagine true coupling could be sweeter than what they share, but it must be for her muscles tighten within as if they are trying to draw something in deeper. She sighs against the futility of her own desires, groping for his erection.

Her fingers close over his hot, stiff member and he groans, a primal sound that reverberates through his chest. How she loves the throaty sounds he makes while she pleasures him. Her fingers caress him lightly as he pushes into the cup of her hand.

Their rhythms match, both swaying into the other's hand, then away, then in again. His fingers slip down to cover the folds of what the goddess holds sacred, and the nub of her desire collides with the base of his palm again and again.

Their rhythm quickens and her hand tightens. Her palm catches the small amount of moisture from the engorged tip and spreads it along the rock-hard length of his manhood. Their breaths sound harsh but come as one, and their heartbeats match. They almost become one another, she thinks, as she nears the bursting point of her pleasure, her hips moving even more quickly against his hand.

He matches her pace, and she feels him grow even harder, that last stiffening just before he is ready to spill his seed. She wishes he could spill within her and create a child, a proof of their everlasting love. But for now, it cannot be.

She cries out as her pleasure is released and her body tingles and grows warm. She feels faint and her legs become weak as wave after wave pours through her body. When she is replete and her hips have stopped grinding against his palm, only then does he push his manhood insistently. She grips him firmly with both hands, but lets him set the pace. He moves back and forth more quickly until the last moments when he strains into the tight circle formed of her hands.

A guttural groan is torn from his throat as his seed spills and she catches every precious drop. When the last shudder racks his body, he sags against her for only a moment drawing in deep, ragged breaths. Bracing himself, he swings her up into his arms and she cradles her head between his jaw and shoulder.

He carries her into their chamber.

The vision ended abruptly, and Lia's hand shook as she lifted the flashlight to reveal an entryway to a chamber—the same chamber where the woman's lover carried her. Lia stumbled across the passageway and over the threshold. She stopped just inside and leaned back against the wall beside the opening. Her whole body trembled, craving something her own hands couldn't satisfy.

She flashed the light around, but the beam revealed an empty room, the floor covered in sand like the passageways.

No statue. She had almost expected to see it there even though according to the glyphs on the scroll, the statue would be situated in a chamber large enough to hold hundreds of people attending the ritual.

Nothing tangible here, but she was overcome with a sense of love and devotion and physical arousal—all the things the woman felt for her lover. Lia slid down the wall to sit at its base, tears streaming down her face. The woman's connection to her lover was a relationship Lia had always wanted but never came close to having.

Before she was aware of what she was doing, she had jammed the handle of the flashlight between her legs, rubbing the long, cylindrical case back and forth. She closed her eyes, moaning . . .

He lays her on the thick pallet he had prepared earlier in anticipation of their tryst.

How often do they not make it to the makeshift bed before their hands pleasure one another's bodies? Too often, she thinks and smiles in the dark. A faint light glimmers from the other side of the small chamber. He has lighted a lamp.

Quickly, she crawls from the soft pallet, over the abrasive sand until she reaches the back chamber wall. There she digs a hole in the loose sand and buries his seed as a gift to the goddess. It will not sprout him sons, she thinks, and stifles a laugh at the image of babies springing from the sand, but they mustn't leave any evidence of what they do behind. And perhaps the goddess will reconsider what she asks the eldest daughter of the king to forsake if she is brought closer to the pleasure a man can give a woman.

Her lover catches her from behind, his strong arm slipping around her stomach. He has discarded his robe and he holds her close to his naked body. She feels his growing manhood press against the back of her thigh. He swings her up and deposits her on the pallet, tumbling along with her. They laugh as limbs tangle and warm skin slides along warm skin.

The faint light is a bright corona outlining him in stark relief as he raises and kneels between her legs, spreading them wide. Her hips surge upward and she longs for him to plunge inside, but it would be certain death for both of them. The royal physician examines her frequently to ensure her maidenhead is intact. It is a humiliating experience that she loathes, and she will be glad to leave it and everything else behind when her lover deems it is time for them to go away together.

She dreams of the day he will be able to pierce her maidenhead and make her feel like a true woman.

He runs his hands from her calves, over her knees, to the sensitive flesh of her inner thighs. She quivers with delight and forgets everything except the feel of his hands on her body.

He lowers his head and his fingers spread her folds farther apart. She sighs with the first exquisite touch of his tongue in the creases around her nub and the tingle of arousal begins. He laps at her gently, long slow strokes that make her squirm into him. His hands move under her hips and clutch her buttocks. His touch is hot and she feels as if the imprints of his large hands have been burned into her flesh. He raises her closer to him, his tongue gliding up and down the rim of the goddess' portal.

Her breath quickens and her heart pounds. Her hips begin a rhythm all their own and his lips return to her nub, surrounding it, suckling it. She pushes into him, her back arching, ready for the rush of sensation, but at the last moment he stops and draws away.

She hangs on the edge of oblivion, poised on the brink of eternity, but instead the feeling recedes a little. He flicks his fingers around her nub a few times, but not enough to send her plummeting over the edge.

"Please, please, Beloved!" she begs in a whimper, her body writhing with need. "Do not stop!"

But it is part of their lovemaking and she enjoys his teasing touch.

"Not yet, my One," he whispers hoarsely. "There are more pleasures to come."

Lia groaned aloud when the vision ended, and she was back in the chamber, alone and horny as hell. She shook her head against the wall and tried to bring the vision back. She wanted to experience what they experienced, wanted to live inside the woman and be loved in a way she had never been loved by a man. To be treasured and wanted, even if the complete act of penetration was an impossibility.

Sobbing, Lia yanked the flashlight from between her legs. No more! It wasn't enough, would never be enough. She had to find the statue. The answer was with the statue. Lia wasn't sure how she knew it. Probably from the woman in the vision. At least, if she found the statue, she could get out of here. If she hadn't found Mac by then, she could go for help.

Lia stood on shaky legs and stepped out into the passageway. She closed her eyes and tried to make her mind go blank again. This time it was easier and she knew where she needed to go and what she had to do.

Half an hour later, she entered a medium-sized chamber. Larger than where the woman and her lover met, but not spacious enough to hold hundreds of worshipers. Here, there was a large block of stone long enough for someone to lie on, its flat surface as tall as her waist. Could it be an altar? Glyphs she didn't know how to read were carved on all sides.

Piles of rubbish lined the side walls. Fragments of papyrus that disintegrated when she touched them. Dull metal tools. Clay vessels that shattered when she tried to move them. But none of this really interested her.

She moved around the slab of rock to the back of the chamber. She found a loose stone and pushed inward. Prepared for grinding, whining gears, she was surprised when a section of the wall moved aside with barely a whisper. The flash of her light revealed a long flight of steps leading down. The steps seemed intact as far as the light would reach. Everything else had held up well over time, no reason these shouldn't have either. She started down.

At the bottom, there was another stone to push and another door to open. Just as she laid her hand on the correct block, everything blurred and she was back again with the woman and her lover.

"More?" she asks in a timid whisper. She doesn't think her body can stand more stimulation, but she knows it can. They shouldn't take so much time tonight, yet she can't bear to tell him she must leave. She prays to the goddess that the guards will not notice her absence.

But will the goddess heed her prayers when they go against everything the priests tell them the goddess stands for?

She cannot believe the goddess would wish her to abstain from this . . . and it is her last thought as her lover's hands grip her waist and pulls her up and toward him. She rises until she is seated on his thighs, her portal of Seniha lying along his thick, hard length. She squirms closer until her nub is in contact with the flesh just above the root of his manhood. She rocks her hips, bumping him just enough to bring back the sweet tingle of anticipation.

Her lover has wrapped his arms around her, to steady her, and his head dips, his mouth closing over the tight peak of one breast. His teeth nip gently and his tongue rakes the hardened flesh, drawing circles around and around. He moves to the other and lavishes the same attention to it. She throws back her head, her hands threaded through his silky hair. She glides her portal back and forth over his stiff manhood, careful not to press too hard although she wants him inside of her so badly tears well in her eyes.

She is almost there, once again on the edge of the precipice, but his hands grasp her hips and he stops her. She trembles violently.

"Beloved, please," she whimpers, tossing her head from side to side. "Please release me from my torment."

"Not yet," he says again and kisses her. His lips taste sweetly of her own dew as his tongue delves into her mouth. Her fingers clench in his hair and her hips thrust toward him, but he holds her firmly away from him.

Time! She wishes it could stand still for them, but it races forward whenever they are together. She has been away much longer than she should have. She only came tonight for a quick kiss and caress. When they brought one another to ecstasy in the passageway, she should have dressed and left right then. But when he swung her up into his arms, she couldn't resist another session of his passion. Now, too much time has passed.

"Beloved," she says as she draws away from his kisses, but flings her arms around him. "I should go back before I am missed. I would rather die a thousand deaths than leave you, but I do not want you in danger."

"Soon," he croons, his warm breath tickling her ear. "Soon we will be together and far away from here. But tonight is for our love."

Gently, he loosens her arms and slips her off his thighs. He lies back on the pallet and she looks at him. His face is in shadow and she cannot see his expression, but his manhood is taut, gently curving upward. Her pulse pounds throughout her body, the drumming echoed in her swollen nub. She moves to her knees beside him and reaches for his enormous length.

"Come here, my One," he says and catches her hand. "We will love one another together."

He indicates for her to straddle him so that her back is to him. He positions her so that her legs are tucked under his shoulders, and his mouth easily finds the center of her pleasure. She moans as his tongue licks greedily at her soft folds. Then she bends and places her hands around his shaft. He stiffens and pushes into her grasp as her mouth covers the engorged head. She rakes her tongue across the tender underside again and again and is teased by the same motions he creates around her nub.

She takes as much of him as she can into her mouth and begins the in-and-out rhythm he enjoys. His lips do the same to her nub as his hands squeeze her buttocks. Soon, she can barely breathe or think as her hips quicken and his lips move faster. Then a fingertip eases just inside the tightness of her anus, massaging in time to their movements, and she is swept away on a wave of bliss. She cries out against his manhood and her excitement ends his torture as well. Warm fluid spurts into her mouth as she rides the crest of sensation that has threatened to tear her asunder.

And then she feels rough hands on her, pulling her off of her lover. She senses more than sees him rolling to his feet, a feral growl on his lips. More hands fasten onto her body, holding her back as she strains to free herself, to reach her lover. The strange hands touch her in places they shouldn't touch. They hold her arms outstretched and her legs far apart. A hand clamps over her wet portal of pleasure.

"Let her go!" her lover snarls, struggling against his captors. "You want me, not her! Free her!"

"On your knees, novice!" The dark and dangerous voice of the Dark Priest commands her lover from beneath his hood.

"No!" she screams. "We have done nothing wrong!"

The robed men who hold her lover drive him to his knees.

"That is for the royal physician to decide," the Dark Priest rasps. He nods and something hard and leathery touches the entry to her portal. Pain rips through as it is forced inside, where only moments before she had felt pure ecstasy. Then she understands.

"NOOOOO!" she screams and cannot stop. "NO NO NO NO NO!"

The destruction of her maidenhead means her death and the death of her lover! It is the only way the Dark Priest can rid himself of her lover and the conspiracy against him.

She is gagged to stifle her tormented screams. Before she is carried away, her lover manages to escape his captors for a brief moment and embraces her one last time.

"Forgive me," he whispers into her ear before they take him away. "Remember, my One . . . forever!"

"Nooooo. . . ." Lia moaned. She was on her knees, her hand lying lightly on the stone block. Tears streamed from her eyes, and her breathing came in hitching gasps. She could hardly bear witnessing the discovery and separation of the lovers. Her heart felt as if it were shattering in her chest.

Lia was left with the terrible feeling that the lovers had never been reunited.

When her breathing had evened and the tears had stopped, only then did she stand on shaky legs and press the block of stone. Like the mechanism at the top of the steps, the doorway opened almost silently. She wiped at her tear-stained face and crossed the threshold.

Immediately, the wall behind her slid together soundlessly. She whirled around and flashed her light over the stone blocks. The stones were almost seamless, and she might not have noticed them at all if she hadn't known they were there.

Lia shone the light around. Like the passages, the floor was layered in sand. To the right was a large archway and to the left was what looked like a crack in the natural rock wall creating a crevice barely wide enough for a person to walk through.

The archway would only take her back to the beginning of the maze. The crevice would take her where she needed to go. As long as she still remembered what she learned while inhabiting the woman in her visions, she could always find the way out. She turned left.

Lia crossed the room then took a step into the crevice, almost expecting the walls to begin to close in on her. She waited, holding her breath, but didn't hear anything. She had to go on if she wanted to find out what all of this was about. She took a few more tentative steps forward, then she was racing along as fast as she could.

The crevice was almost straight, veering neither to the left or right. She ran until the stitch in her side caught again, and she was forced to slow.

Where could Mac be? she thought guiltily. It had been a long while since he and his whereabouts had crossed her mind. She had gotten so caught up in the drama in her visions that she had allowed it to push aside what should have been her main concern.

Minutes passed like hours before she saw a faint light in the distance. The end of the crevice was near. She limped the last few steps out of the crevice and into the Chamber of Zamar.

The huge cavern could be nothing else.

The walls shimmered with a gentle glow that lighted the entire chamber. She blinked against the sudden light after hours of darkness and took two more steps into the huge chamber.

A temblor moved through the rock, and she felt the reverberation throughout her body. She turned in time to see the walls settle into place, only a thin line marking where the crevice had been.

Lia knew she should panic, but she didn't as she waited for another set of moving gears to create another opening. Long minutes passed, but nothing happened. No new exit was created.

She was trapped. She didn't know the way out of the chamber. What knowledge she had gained from the woman didn't cover how to escape the chamber, only how to find it.

A thought suddenly made her feel guiltier. What if Mac had discovered one of these silent passages that closed as soon as he stepped through? She should have looked beyond the row of boulders, searched the wall for a thin line that indicated the secret opening.

But there had been no footprints in the sand. How could he have possibly reached an opening without stepping onto the sand?

Lia took a deep breath. First things first. Find out what had compelled her to come to this chamber, then find a way out. She remembered the way back to the cavern where Mac had disappeared. She could find it again and do another, more thorough search. Right now, she had to find out if the statue was here.

She slowly walked farther into the chamber. Three times or more as large as the cavern where Mac had disappeared, it could easily accommodate a small village to witness a religious rite.

Lia switched off her flashlight.

The floor was bare rock. A large pool had been cut into the center of the rock floor, its perfect circular shape obviously made by man, not developed naturally. A round "island" of rock had been left in the center of the pool and had been carved into a pyramid shape rising thirty feet in the air. Steps on the two sides that she could see led to a small platform at the top, and the silhouette of—

Lia started. For an instant, she thought someone stood motionless on the flat peak looking down at her. Then she realized it was a statue and its back was turned toward her—the statue of Zamar.

The tragedy of the lovers in the vision had put a halt to the overwhelming sexual need raging within, but the sight of the statue stirred the need all over again. Her knees grew weak and she trembled all over. Her clit throbbed in time to her steps as she approached the pool. She felt as if she were almost in a daze she couldn't shake off.

It took only moments to shed her clothing. Nude, she stepped into the shallow depth and walked until the level reached her breasts. The water was cool and clear. She swam a few strokes, then treaded water as she loosened her hair. She rinsed away the sweat and grit of the past few hours. Then she swam to the island, reveling in the feel of the water gliding over her skin and between her legs. She climbed out on the island.

Lia walked all the way around the pyramid and found the other two sides identical to the first two she'd seen. She stopped when she reached the side the statue faced.

She shivered. The swim had left her refreshed but chilled. However, she thought the shiver really came from what she would find at the top of the pyramid.

The steps were hand-hewn and uniform. She placed one foot on the bottom step and climbed.

The statue's head came into view first and her breath caught. It was the most beautiful likeness of a man she had ever seen— high, flat cheekbones, straight nose, tapered jaw, and a sensuous mouth, lips parted as if he were about to speak. His eyelids were half-closed over two green jewels for irises and inlaid obsidian or jet for pupils. Thick waves of hair swept away from his brow to fall carelessly down his back.

Lia's pulse pounded in her ears. She climbed a few more steps in breathless anticipation.

Straining muscles delineated his neck and broad shoulders. His arms were outstretched toward her, bent at elbow and wrist to suggest he was holding a woman close. Broad chest narrowed to trim waist and slim hips and an erect penis.

Lia stopped short and gasped, pressing her thighs together. This was what she wanted, craved, needed like nothing she'd ever needed before. She hurried up the last few steps.

The statue was over six feet tall, every detail in correct proportion, nothing exaggerated, not even the genitalia. The thick penis jutted out and slightly curved upward, ready to be mounted.

The word shook her. *Mounted* was such a base, primal word. Yet what was sex but the most base and primal act in which two people could engage.

Without thinking, she reached out a finger and ran it along the hard length of his cock.

Lia thought she felt a tremor pass through it, but more likely it was the echo of her own trembling. She licked her lips and ran her fingers over the fine musculature of his flat stomach and chest. She found his nipples, tiny granules of stone that didn't threaten to break off.

She looked up into his jewel-green eyes and wondered what kind of sacrifices he had seen. Were virgins slaughtered before his eyes? Or brutally raped by mortal men who had assumed the persona of the god Zamar?

Lia examined the floor around him, but there were no bloodstains. The actual sacrifice could have taken place elsewhere, perhaps the pool. She turned her attention back to him and eased into the embrace of his arms. His stone flesh was cool against her heated skin.

"You are Zamar," she whispered, her lips close to his as she stood on tiptoe. His erection nudged her belly and she stretched a little farther until the tip of his shaft was wedged in the juncture of her legs.

Her blood pounded in her ears, and she burned where he touched her. She was careful not to put too much weight on his penis, afraid it might snap off. She didn't want to mar this perfect man-statue.

She shifted her weight to spread her legs, noticing the difference in temperature between the cooler stone beneath her feet and where the statue touched her body now. Perhaps her own body heat had warmed the stone.

His cock felt too good against her. She closed her eyes and rubbed back and forth until her hips thrust of their own will. Her hands gripped his shoulders tightly, and she writhed until the tip of his cock was pressed firmly against her clit. She shuddered violently, trying to find release, but couldn't.

"Zamar!" she cried out his name in a breathless rush, as if he were her lover. "I have to, don't I?"

Lia rubbed once more and shuddered again. Her breasts burned in anticipation. She massaged the rigid nipples, which only deepened her need, and wished Zamar's hands were touching her instead. She pretended her hands were his.

While one hand pinched a nipple, the other slipped across her rib cage and over her belly to the mat of curls. She raised her head and looked directly into Zamar's jewel-green eyes. The hand slid against her swollen, wet folds. Fingers caressed her labia lightly in a circular motion until one brushed her clit. Her body arched, aching to be released from this torture. The fingers found her clit again and pressed closer, quickening the motion. It wasn't enough and she quivered with the shock of the thought that had struck her as soon as she saw his hard cock.

Lia removed her hands and placed her body within his embrace, so that his arms surrounded her and his hands braced her back. She stood on tiptoe and raised one leg. She coated her fingers with her juice and spread it over the tip of his cock to make entry easier.

Taking a deep breath, she eased herself over him. Would she freeze as she had always done with live men? Or was this what she had been meant to do all along? She forced herself down, easily, gently, prepared for the panic to seize her and cause her to withdraw.

Nothing happened except a sharp stab of pain when her hymen broke. She hesitated but the pain dissolved. The stone cock was warm inside her, not cool as she expected. It almost felt pliable as she slid farther down, a fraction of an inch at a time, careful to angle her body just right. She was eager to do this, but not at the risk of damaging herself.

She wrapped her arms around his broad shoulders and pushed down, down until he filled her up and her clit was pressed firmly against the angle where his penis joined below his belly. A sigh escaped her lips at the satisfactory fullness of his cock.

She thought there would be more pain, the rock chafing her vagina, but she felt nothing except pleasure. It felt as if he pulsed within her, almost thrusting with her as she began to undulate her hips. *My imagination*, she thought, closing her eyes and pressing her breasts to his, nipple to nipple. Warmth and pleasure surged through her.

She lifted one leg then the other, placing them around his narrow hips, her heels digging into his buttocks. Strong hands gripped her under her arms and helped her increase the rhythmic momentum.

Suddenly, she was aware of heavy breathing in her ear and warm lips on her neck. Powerful thrusts from beneath carried her closer and closer to the edge. She managed to think one clear thought before tumbling over: *I'm dreaming!*

She ground herself against warm flesh, arching her back as the most powerful orgasm she'd ever felt struck, ricocheting through every limb and nerve. She shuddered and shivered and screamed out his name, *"Zamar!"*

He groaned, a ragged sound deep in his throat, and he strained into her, his thrusts deeper and longer. He stiffened and moaned and shook as a hotness burned inside her vagina with his release.

What a wonderful fantasy, Lia thought, brought on by the visions she had experienced. Perhaps another vision, one that seemed more real than the others.

Slowly, she became aware of her hands clenched in thick, silky hair and arms moving around her to hold her up since the shriveling shaft no longer gave support.

Lia jerked back and looked into jewel-green eyes that looked back at her.

"My One," he said, his voice husky and rich.

THREE

He was even more handsome than before as his eyes searched her face and his full lips curved into a smile. His skin, now the color of bronze, glistened with sweat.

Lia gasped. "It's—It's not possible! You can't be alive!"

He laughed and the sound rumbled in his chest. "I am Zamar. You called my name and sacrificed yourself to me. Of course, I am alive. And you are my One."

"Nooooo," Lia moaned. "You're only a legend, and—"

"Legend? I?" He laughed again, and started down the ancient hewn steps. His arms tightened around her, holding her securely.

When he reached the bottom of the steps, he walked into the water until it lapped at his waist. Carefully, he laid her back until she was submerged to her neck, her body floating before him. One arm still supported her. The refreshing water eased the soreness between her thighs.

"I—I'm not your One," Lia said softly, wishing she were his One so she could be loved like the woman in her visions.

He only smiled at her. Cupping his hand and filling it with water, he let the cool liquid trickle over her flushed face.

"Where are the witnesses?"

"Witnesses?"

"Always, the entire village has borne witness to the sacrifice," he explained. "Even if the village is at war, the women and the priests should be in attendance."

Lia ran a hand over his ribs and chest. Touching him and being held by him was as natural as breathing . . . after she'd gotten over the initial shock of finding herself impaled on a live man instead of a stone statue.

"I'm sorry, Zamar. I don't know how to explain. Your people are long gone and all that remains are a few passages in an old book. And a scroll."

"They are gone?" he asked but expected no answer. His dark eyebrows furrowed and a deep sadness filled his eyes. "So it was foretold that one day this would happen. I did not think it would be so soon."

"It's been thousands of years since it happened, whatever it was that wiped out your people. There is so little information about you that it took years for my friend to find this place. And only then because he had a scroll."

"A scroll?"

"A map of this place and how to find it."

Zamar's hand moved to her hair and picked up a strand that was not yet wet. "I have never seen hair the color of gold. Where are you from? What are you now called?"

He worded the question strangely, but she answered. "My

name is Lia Morgan. It's been a long time since the last sacrifice, and the world has changed so much."

"Lia," he said, savoring the sounds, and nodded. "I am aware of the changes though I do not always know what they mean."

"When my friend found a short passage in a book about the Zamarians, the only name your people are known by, he became obsessed over the idea of finding this place and the sacrificial chamber of the god Zamar."

"I am no god! I am as mortal as you."

"Then how did you become a statue?"

"The Dark Priest punished me when I conspired against him."

A spike of fear shot through her and she shivered. The Dark Priest was the one who ordered the destruction of the woman's maidenhead so she and her lover would be sentenced to death.

"Do you re—" Zamar broke off and hesitated. Then he said, "Do you know of him?"

Lia nodded, but he seemed to sense her fear. He gathered her up into his arms and cradled her as he sat at the edge of the pool. She clung to him, feeling safer with his arms around her.

"Ever since I entered this place, I've had visions of a man and woman. I saw everything through the eyes of the woman as she met her lover, although it was forbidden for her to make love. They—They were caught by the Dark Priest, and . . ."

"And?" he prompted.

"And the woman was—was deflowered at the order of the Dark Priest, so the two lovers would be executed." Lia shrugged. "That's all. That was the last of the visions before I found this chamber."

Zamar leaned close to her and whispered into her ear, *"Remember, my One . . . forever."*

Trembling, Lia looked up at him and tears filled her eyes. "Those were his last words to her, the last words I heard, anyway. He was always in the darkness and the shadows and I never saw his face. It really was you?"

"Yes," he murmured against her hair.

"And the woman?"

"She was Aeliha. As the eldest daughter of the king, her body was sacred to the goddess we worshipped at the time. She was forbidden the pleasures of the flesh, especially intimacy with a man. I became a priest because I could not marry my Aeliha and to try to learn to control my passions. If I could not have her, I did not want anyone."

"But you were together anyway."

He smiled. "We could not stay away from one another. Aeliha would slip past her guards and come to me here in the priests' chambers, although I begged her not to."

"Wh-What happened to her?"

Zamar looked down at her and placed a kiss on her lips. "I will tell you later."

"Why?"

"I do not think you are ready to rem—to hear."

Lia jerked upright and would have leapt from his embrace, but he held her tightly.

"I know the word you keep stumbling over! Why should I *remember* anything?" Lia shook her head. "I was in the woman's mind, and I could see out of her eyes. I know some things, but I don't know everything she knew."

Zamar pulled her back down to sit in his lap, his arms around her. Why did it feel so right to be with him like this? She couldn't find the strength to leave his embrace. She didn't really want to. She wanted his hands on her body, his lips against hers. She wanted him to make love to her again.

"I had the impression that you would die when the Dark Priest found you two together. The woman kept thinking it would mean your deaths if you were discovered. Why were you not killed?"

"I was punished with a fate worse than death," Zamar murmured sadly. "I was only a novice priest. In the very beginning I saw how he controlled even the eldest priests. I wanted to believe he had good intentions for our people, but I soon came to realize his plans were only for the good of Mahkul."

"M-Mahkul?"

"The Dark Priest's name was Mahkul. He wanted the power to control and the wealth the people would give him. When I would not betray my people and led the conspiracy to stop him, Mahkul found a way to stop me. Instead of allowing me to be executed as I should have been, he cast me in stone. The curse showed the people how powerful Mahkul was, and they eagerly followed him."

As he spoke, his hand lazily caressed her breasts until her nipples were hard points. Desire stirred in her once again, although she wouldn't have thought it was possible so soon.

"Over time, they began to believe the lies Mahkul told them. Every generation when the sacrifice of a virgin was made, I saw they were ever further removed from the old ways and enslaved to Mahkul's ways. It began with the abandonment of Seniha, the goddess my people had worshipped since the beginning of time. I believe it amused Mahkul to make me as a god in the eyes of my people."

His hand roved farther down over her ribs and belly, a finger rimming her navel. She quivered at his touch even as she listened to him.

"I would try to tell them, but they would not listen. Even though they were told I was their god brought to life, they feared Mahkul more than they feared me. After all, I was only alive for one day every generation, but they were forced to live with his greed for power and wealth every day of their lives. And I never showed them any powers I might possess."

"And the virgin sacrifice?" Lia asked, her voice trembling. Suddenly, she was afraid this Dark Priest would appear and drive a knife through her heart. Although, technically, she was no longer a virgin.

"The sacrifice is her virginity, not her life," he said with a small smile, as if he knew what she was thinking. "We would spend a day and a night in intimacy, hoping she would conceive. If she didn't, Mahkul would banish her from the village, never to be seen again. When I was brought to life the next time, I would sometimes see the grown son or daughter that resulted from the previous union. Sometimes there would be none," he added wistfully.

Lia's eyes grew wide. Conception was a concern with them, but it was much too late to worry about it. She had never dreamed the statue would actually come alive while inside her. Or maybe she did, but didn't want to admit it. She decided they would worry about it later—if there was a later. Their first priority was escape.

"Is there another way out of here?" she asked as his hand moved even lower, fingers tangling in the curls between her thighs. "The crevice closed when I entered."

"It has always done so when the virgin entered this chamber. Always, when the night was over, the crevice would open and the people would leave, and I would become a statue until the next generation."

"You would be intimate in front of everyone?" she asked, trying to imagine performing as she had in front of hundreds of people. But she supposed that was the least of their worries.

Zamar laughed, his green eyes twinkling. "No, not after the first mounting."

Lia started. There was that word again, *mounting*. A word she had never thought of in connection with sex before today. Had it been left over from a suppressed memory of the woman's?

"A tent would be prepared for us and we would spend our time there while the people feasted and rejoiced. A successful mating ensured a bountiful generation for the village."

His finger delved deeper, driving into her and her breath caught. Her hips pushed against him so that his finger would go even deeper. Too soon he pulled out, setting her on the edge of the pool so that she was half in, half out of the water. He parted her legs and moved between them. His hands raised her hips and his head lowered.

His tongue swirled over the folds and creases and dipped into her slit. She leaned back, closing her eyes, and let the sensations wash over her. He sucked her clit, intensifying the urgency, bringing her to the edge, then stopped and circled it with his tongue again. He had teased the woman in this same manner, and she had loved it. Lia now knew exactly why.

Zamar repeated this process over and over, driving her wild with the build up and let down again and again. He continued until she was squirming with the need of release, bucking her hips toward his mouth only to find it gone.

"Oh, Zamar, please," Lia whispered when she didn't think she could stand another minute of his sweet torture. Lia gasped when he slowly eased a fingertip into her anus, but her muscle gripped him hard and pleasure rippled through her. Other fingers slid deep into her slit, a wonderful feeling she could now enjoy. Then his mouth sealed over her clit, his tongue working it quickly.

The myriad sensations all at once sent her over the edge, her hips moving in a frenzy against his lips and hand, as her muscles tightened and a tidal wave of pleasure swept through her. When the last tingling ebbed away, she relaxed, totally depleted.

She didn't resist when he turned her over and stepped between her legs again. She couldn't have resisted if she wanted. She lay still as he spread her legs farther and entered her from behind, his stiff cock sliding easily into her. It occurred to Lia that they didn't have to do this because there was no village to ensure fertility and bounty for. Everything and everyone Zamar had known was gone. But as she languidly joined the rhythm he'd set, his cock pumping into her, she didn't see any reason to stop him either. What was done, was done. Lia had no regrets. She didn't really regret that Mac hadn't been her first. She didn't regret sacrificing her virginity to Zamar and releasing him from his prison of stone.

He grew longer and harder within her, and his thrusts increased in speed and intensity. She tried to keep up, but she was exhausted. When she thought he might batter her into pulp, he came with a loud groan, shooting his hot semen into her. Instinctively, she pressed back against him, hoping her movements prolonged his pleasure. He made a few last jerking motions, then collapsed atop her, carrying most of his weight on his arms on each side of her. He kissed the nape of her neck.

"I have waited an eternity for this, my One," he whispered.

Lia shook her head. She was not his One, as much as she wished it were true. She opened her mouth to deny it, but he kissed her instead.

"There is another way out," he said. "Mahkul would appear and disappear at will, but it was not by conjure. He had uncovered a few secrets, including how to turn a man to stone, but that was the extent of his sorcery. He had very little natural ability and it was another reason he hated me."

Lia let the opportunity to deny she was his One slip by and focused on his belief there was another way out of the chamber. "That's wonderful!"

"But I do not know where it is," he said regretfully.

"That's not wonderful," she said, trying to keep the disappointment from her tone.

"We will find it." He rose up and helped her to her feet. They swam across to the other side and emerged near Lia's belongings.

"Maybe we should just wait until the crevice opens again," Lia suggested as she got dressed, and pulled her wet hair into a ponytail.

Zamar shook his head, his coal-black hair rippling over his shoulders. "With the dawn, the crevice opens and I begin to turn to stone. It is a much slower process than coming alive. I grow sluggish then I cannot walk. Soon I do not blink or breathe and I lose consciousness of my surroundings. I tried to escape several times in the beginning, but I would always turn to stone. I found it was easier for the sacrifice if I chose an accommodating position before I turned completely."

"But then it doesn't matter, does it? Even if we find a way out, you would still turn to stone. We can just wait until—until the time is up and the crevice opens." Lia finished tucking her shirt into the waistband of her shorts, but her heart was crumbling in her chest. She had finally found the one man who could get past her panic and allow her to make love like a normal person, only to lose him. She could never bring him back again because she was no longer a virgin.

"No, it does matter. If Mahkul controls the openings then he is here, somewhere."

"That's not possible, is it? He would be long dead."

"Immortality was one of the few secrets Mahkul learned. He had uncovered ancient paintings—ancient even in our time— deep in the caves beneath this one. He was the only one who knew where they were located. Most of the paintings had been defaced, their meanings undecipherable. But a few, he said, remained intact. From them he learned the secret of immortality and how to turn a man to stone and a few other tricks to impress and control the people. He did not have the ability to expand on the knowledge he had gleaned and create his own conjures."

"Immortality," Lia whispered incredulously. Yet, was immortality any more unbelievable than a stone statue turning into a live man? And if the Dark Priest was *here*, was he the one who had taken Mac?

"He could very well be watching us now," Zamar said, his eyes darting toward the shadowy reaches of the chamber's farthest depths.

Lia hugged herself, glad she had dressed. Her skin crawled with the thought of the Dark Priest's eyes on her. Her face grew warm with the thought that he might have seen what she'd done with Zamar the statue and Zamar the man.

The faintest whisper of a sound echoed throughout the cavern and startled them both. Footsteps sounded and a brilliant light moved from behind the pyramid and around the pool.

Zamar stepped in front of her protectively, but she peeked over his shoulder, blinking against the light. The footsteps stopped several dozen yards away and the light went out. It took a few moments for Lia's eyes to adjust to the sudden dimness, but when she did . . .

"Mac!" she cried out and launched herself around Zamar, running toward him.

In the next instant, Zamar threw his arm around her midsection, bringing her up short, and called out, "Mahkul!"

Zamar held her tight against him. "This is your friend?"

Lia nodded weakly.

"This is also Mahkul, the Dark Priest," he said softly.

FOUR

"No . . . no . . ." she mewled, her mind racing, trying to put the pieces together and resisting at the same time. She closed her eyes, but wasn't swept away into a vision. Yet, scenes flashed before her eyes . . . Zamar bound and gagged at the top of the pyramid. She, as the woman in the visions, on her knees, her arms trussed behind her. Mac as the Dark Priest standing to one side, the light of triumph in his eyes, his mouth almost smiling. The flash of a blade toward her, horror in Zamar's eyes, then . . . blackness . . . but everything to her was crystal clear.

Lia jerked her eyes open. "You," she said, her voice hoarse. "You brought me here on purpose."

"Of course, Lia," he said, moving closer, and it was then she noticed the gun in his hand. "I've spent many lifetimes looking for you. I knew who you were from the moment we met, and the similarity of your names clinched it. Those who are reborn often have names similar to those in a previous life. You're remembering, aren't you?"

Lia nodded.

"Good."

"You forged the map," Lia said, trying to untangle her thoughts. "And the book. To lure me here with you."

Mac laughed. "Well, technically, it's not a forgery. I drew the map centuries ago. The book is legitimate, too. I was working with the archaeologist during the time he wrote it. The hardest part has been finding you, Aeliha. This is the first time our paths have crossed since I witnessed your beheading."

Zamar's hands tightened around her, and she could feel the tension and hatred emanating from him.

"That you were still a virgin when we met was miraculous," Mac continued. "Only a virgin fucking the statue could bring Zamar back to life. Do you know how rare virgins are these days? If I'd known how difficult it would be to find one, I'd have changed the circumstances of his turning. But there you were, Aeliha, ripe for the plucking."

"Why do you need Zamar alive? I know you hate him. You could have smashed the statue into a million bits at any time and that would have taken care of him forever. Why did you need *me*? Any virgin would have done at any time before now."

"I knew you were out there, somewhere, Aeliha. I didn't know it would take so many lifetimes to find you or I might have given up sooner. When our people were conquered and slaughtered, I could have smashed the statue and been rid of him for all time. But I had to have a purpose, didn't I? Immortality can be a bitch without a purpose. Besides, I wanted to see the look on his face when I killed you in front of him again. I want to see the loss and despair. And then I want to see the look on his face when I kill him."

Lia whirled away from Mac's laughter to face Zamar. "The thing in his hand is a weapon. If he pulls the trigger, the small handle, a little piece of metal will come out so fast you won't be able to see it, but it can kill you if it hits you."

Zamar jerked his head to show he understood and shoved her behind him again. "Mahkul, let her leave this place and we will settle our differences."

Mac shook his head. "I can't do that. While I was working with the archaeologist, I found an incantation to take another's power, but it requires the sacrifice of a woman. Not necessarily a virgin, Lia, but you will have to die this time."

"Oh, Mac . . ." Lia began but didn't know what to say. The memories of Aeliha were blending, then receding, separating with the memories of her life as Lia. Aeliha's memories were almost as full of Mahkul as Zamar, especially when they were children. If she was Aeliha, how could she have been so easily tricked by him as Lia?

"I really will miss you, Lia. Some of the best times I've had in this millennium were with you." Mac shifted his gaze to Zamar. "You, I won't miss at all."

Mac eased his backpack off, reached in and brought out a pair of plastic handcuffs.

"Cuff him," Mac said and threw the straps at Lia.

Time slowed. As Lia watched, the cuffs made a lazy arc in the space between them. Mac's and Zamar's movements became sluggish, and when Mac spoke, his voice was guttural and drawn-out so that she couldn't understand what he said.

Lia stood, her heart pounding in her chest, her breath harsh and fast. Had she done this? If so, all she had to do was pluck the gun from Mahkul's hand. The effort to step forward was almost too great. She wasn't in slow motion, but her legs felt as if dead weights had been tied to them.

She pushed on, her heart beating faster, her breath turning ragged. She had almost reached Mahkul when they were all in sync again and time moved naturally. Mahkul gasped but reacted more quickly than she could. He reached for her.

With a sudden burst of energy and knowledge, she dodged him easily. In a rapid double strike, she knocked the gun from his hand and backhanded a blow across his arrogant sneer.

Mahkul barely flinched. He grabbed her by the hair, fingers digging into the base of her ponytail, and slung her to her knees. Another quick movement and the gun was back in his hand, the barrel jammed into the side of her neck.

It had all happened so quickly and smoothly that Zamar could only take a couple of steps toward them.

"I'll kill her," Mahkul threatened, the words stopping Zamar as effectively as a blow. "She's served her purpose by bringing you back. I thought it would be amusing, the three of us together again, but I don't really need her."

"If you kill her, you will have to kill me," Zamar said.

"Maybe," Mahkul conceded. "Believe me, I would regret it. I only waited this long in the hopes Aeliha would return. But I won't have to kill you, Zamar. A well-placed bullet will take you down without killing you."

Zamar's fists clenched at his side. "What do you want?" he ground out.

"What I've always wanted. Your power."

Zamar shook his head. "If there was a way, I would have gladly given it to you when we were children. You were jealous of it then, the talent Aeliha and I had. There is no way to transfer the power we are born with and you know this."

Mahkul chuckled. "That's the incantation I found. A few special words and the death of a woman. And, naturally, it results in the death of the one with the power. My talent has always been in spell work, remember? I could always manifest the most complicated and intricate of incantations."

Zamar said nothing, but he'd brought his clenched fist up in front of him.

"We're wasting time. Pick up the cuffs, slowly, and give them to Aeliha."

No! The word exploded in Lia's mind. She had to do something to stop him. They were going to die anyway. If she could incapacitate Mahkul somehow, it would give Zamar time to escape. He might not get far before dawn and again turned to stone, but it would complicate matters for Mahkul. He would have to wait until the next generation and find another virgin sacrifice. By then, she could be reborn again, an adult, and find a way to stop him.

Determined to save Zamar, energy welled within her again. She focused and concentrated. She leapt straight up, throwing Mahkul off-balance, and caught his wrists. The ease and agility of her movements surprised her. She had the grace of a cat.

"Go, Zamar!" she shouted as she struggled to keep Mahkul's arms in the air and the gun's aim away from Zamar. She was losing her focus, but Zamar had to leave now. "Go while you can. We'll be together again, I promise!"

"No, it ends here. Move away, Aeliha."

The surge of strength was waning. Oh, why couldn't she hold onto the energy within her? "Zamar, please go. I-I can't hold him much longer."

As the last of her strength slipped away, Mahkul overcame her. He tossed her high into the air, toward the nearest wall. She knew she was going to crash, breaking every bone in her body, but she couldn't—

She jerked to a halt as if a wire attached to her waist had been snapped short. She floated in midair unsteadily, but she didn't drop like a stone. With only a little effort she pivoted, slowly uprighting herself, and looked at the two men who stood a few yards from one another. Just as Mahkul swung the gun around, Zamar's arm jetted forward, a streak of intense blue lightning leaving his fingertips. The air crackled with the energy and when the bolt touched Mahkul, he became immobile, a web of bright blue currents playing all over his body.

Lia started to take a step, but remembered she was in midair, only to look down and find she had already landed lightly on her feet. She ran to Zamar.

Now, Zamar's hands were several inches apart. Red and orange flames coalesced into a sphere, the size of a golf ball, between his palms.

"Mahkul bound my powers before casting me in stone, but over the undisturbed centuries I have been able to increase the strength of my sorcery," he explained quickly. Sweat beaded on his brow with the effort. "Help me, Aeliha."

"What do I do?" Lia cried out helplessly. Having the memories of Aeliha come at random then leave her completely was frustrating.

"Concentrate, Aeliha," Zamar said softly, patiently. The sphere was almost the size of a tennis ball now. "Remember when we were children, we did this often. We would conjure a fireball, no larger than the tip of a thumb. When we threw it, the blast would bring the palace guards running. We would be sitting, playing in the dirt, and pretend we didn't hear a thing."

Lia smiled and nodded. How many times had her father lectured them against teasing the guards? Too many and they never listened. She glanced at Mahkul. The blue current had lessened.

"Hurry, Aeliha, or the conjure on Mahkul will wear off before we can finish."

Lia stepped in front of Zamar and placed her hands over and under the small sphere, palms inward. She focused her energy on the flickering flames, concentrating on making it bigger, brighter, stronger. The sphere grew rapidly and when it was the size of a basketball, Zamar nodded. Lia carefully removed her hands and backed away. Zamar launched the sphere.

The fireball hit just as the blue charge went out and Mahkul regained mobility. His scream rent the air, his body writhing in the flames until his flesh melted away and he was nothing more than blackened bones. The flames flickered out, leaving a gray skeleton. All was still for a moment, then the skeletal frame collapsed into a heap of ash around the melted lump of the revolver.

Lia turned her back on what was left of Mahkul, tears filling her eyes with grief and sorrow. Zamar gathered her into his arms.

"I remember everything now," she sniffled against his broad chest. "At first, I thought Aeliha was using me to reach you, but now that I remember everything, I know I *am* Aeliha."

"Then you remember—"

"About Mahkul? Yes, he was my brother." She looked up into Zamar's jewel-green eyes, but saw no triumph, only grief and a sorrow to match her own. "When we were children, you and Mahkul were the best of friends. He wasn't always like this, was he?"

Zamar shook his head. "No, not always. But as we grew older, he could not understand why the son of the king had lesser powers than the son of a scribe."

"It's why my father fostered you, to train you as a warrior. He recognized your potential, and he spoke of it often. Maybe too often," she added, thinking of Mahkul's jealousy. "He was furious when you chose the priesthood."

"I went through the ceremony in secret. Not even the king could rescind it once I was sworn in as a novice. Mahkul made the arrangements. Not out of friendship, but as a way to defy his father."

His large hands framed her face. "Warriors were required to marry, but priests were not. Powerful warriors were expected to breed powerful sons for a future army. I could never love another as I loved you. You could not bear my sons and so I did not want sons. It is why I chose the priesthood."

"I remember why! I couldn't stay away from you. I would use my ability to levitate to evade the guards." Lia pressed closer to him, savoring the feel of him in her arms once again. "I remember how I loved you and I still love you with all my heart. I refused to be reborn until I was strong enough to fight Mahkul, too. My bond with Mahkul stayed with me all this time, and I was aware when he found the incantation to steal your power. I knew when he started losing patience and it was time to return. I didn't think my memories would be so deeply repressed in this incarnation. Mahkul recognized me, though. By bringing me here, he forced me to remember. He wanted me to know who I had been and who he was and what he'd done to us."

Zamar lowered his head and kissed her. "Your physical body is different, but you are my Aeliha, my One."

"Forever," she said, but a question had risen to the surface of her consciousness. "Even if we find a way to get out of here, will you still turn into a statue?"

"I believe now that Mahkul is dead, the curse is broken. We will find out at dawn."

Lia glanced at her watch. "We only have a few hours left. What if—"

Zamar laid his finger across her lips. "Shhh, my One. What will be, will be. If I turn to stone, I trust you will find a way to remove the curse."

"If you turn to stone, I'll die!" Lia cried out, tears streaming from her eyes. "I've waited too long. _We_ have waited too long to be together."

Zamar gently wiped the wet trails from her cheeks. "What is another generation when we have waited many hundreds of generations?"

"We shouldn't have to wait," Lia whispered hoarsely.

"No, we should not," he agreed solemnly. "But we will if we must. Now, we have to find how Mahkul entered this chamber so that you will be able to leave if I do turn to stone."

Lia shook her head, but she knew he was right. Only if she was able to leave would she be able to find out how to break the curse and save Zamar. If what Zamar believed was true, it didn't matter. But if the curse wasn't broken with Mahkul's death, then they had to be prepared.

Zamar took her hand to walk with her around the pool, when she stumbled over Mahkul's backpack. She knelt and rummaged through it. He had kept an extra set of clothes, khaki shirt and shorts, and she handed them to Zamar.

Lia glanced up at him. "As much as I love you just the way you are, you might want to put these on. If the curse is broken, you'll need them anyway. They should fit."

They did. Nicely, Lia thought. Mahkul wasn't quite as large as Zamar and they were snug. He couldn't button the shirt over his broad chest, so he tucked the ends in the waistband of his shorts. He slung the backpack over his shoulders after watching the way she put on hers.

They backtracked around the pool, going in the direction from which Mahkul had come. His footprints seemed to emerge from the wall where no opening was in evidence. Lia examined the stone wall closely and found the hairline crack outlining the doorway. She pointed it out to Zamar.

"There must be a way to open it from here," he said.

They pressed the wall near the crack and a small stone, its outline all but invisible, moved beneath Zamar's touch. The large section of stone swung back with barely a whisper.

Lia turned on her flashlight. The passageway was small and cramped, sand and gravel littering the floor. It turned to the right. She hesitated. What if Mahkul had set traps?

"We have no choice, Aeliha," Zamar murmured as if he could read her mind. Hadn't it always been so? He knew what she felt almost before she began feeling it.

She nodded and stepped inside, Zamar close behind, his hand reassuringly on her shoulder. They had only gone a few paces when the doorway slid shut behind them, leaving them in total darkness except for the beam from her flashlight.

"I never knew about this passageway," Zamar said softly as they followed its curve to the right.

If Lia's calculations were correct, this passageway was circling around the large chamber. They stepped over stones and sank in deep drifts of sand until at last the flashlight illuminated a stone wall in front of them. It took less than a minute to find the small stone in the wall that triggered the opening.

The door of stone swung open and they stepped into a medium sized chamber, covered in a layer of sand . . . and footprints! Lia flashed the light around. There was an archway to the left, but the walls, directly across from them and to the right were solid. Yet footprints led to both walls.

"I recognize this room," Lia said. "To the right is where the crevice opened."

"This is the antechamber, yes," Zamar commented. "The villagers entered through the arch. It leads back to where they entered the caves from the other side."

"I entered from there," Lia said and flashed her light at the wall directly across from them. "It leads up to a small room with an altar."

"Mahkul's chamber," Zamar said.

Once again, they easily found the stone to press to open the doorway. They ascended the long flight of steps and emerged behind the altar. They didn't linger, but left the room and followed the passageways until they reached the main one, pale moonlight showing them the exit to outside. Lia reached it first and turned to watch Zamar step into the fresh air for the first time in millennia.

He stood, bathed in moonlight, his face turned to the starry sky. He wore an incredible smile.

Lia didn't want to, but she checked her watch. Just over an hour until dawn. Although the night had been long and tiring, she was overcome with how quickly they were running out of time. If Mahkul's death didn't break the curse, then how was she to go on? She was as much Aeliha now as Lia. She loved Zamar. How could she bear to let him go?

"The stars are not as bright," Zamar said.

"Air pollution," Lia explained. "We've managed to mess up the planet quite a bit since your time."

He nodded and looked at her.

"This is it," Lia whispered. "In about an hour, we'll know whether you turn to stone or not."

"If I do—"

"If you do, then I have to find a way to bring you back permanently. It could take many lifetimes, but I'll do it!" she swore, tears filling her eyes. She took a step toward him, but he swept forward and enclosed her in his arms.

Zamar kissed her tears away. "I pray to Seniha that with Mahkul's death the curse is broken. With many conjures it is so."

Lia nodded. "I pray you're right. We've waited so long, I don't know how I'll go on."

"I'll wait for you," he said with a smile.

"You'll have no choice!" Lia laughed, but it was a nervous, giddy sound.

"Come," he said, taking her hand. "We'll watch the sun rise together."

She let him lead her to the flat rock where millennia ago she had waited to enter the caverns to be with Zamar for what turned out to be their last time together, and only hours ago she had stood watching the desert devour the sun. She had been two different people who were now blended into one—one who loved Zamar.

"I don't want to let you go, Beloved," she whispered and slipped into his embrace. He held her protectively and she looped her arms around his neck, hugging him tightly. She could feel the quick beating of his heart in his chest and his warm breath near her ear.

"I will not be far, my One," he promised softly. "Only a heartbeat away whenever you think of me. I will be thinking of you as well."

Zamar's head bent and his mouth closed over hers. His lips were so familiar to her now, as was his touch. His hands slid down the small of her back and into the waistband of her shorts. Raw need pulsed through her, throbbing in her breasts and clit. Trembling, she loosened her arms from around his neck and trailed her fingers over his smooth chest. She knew his body, every ridge and contour, and traced them with her fingertips. His nipples were hard points, and her lips surrounded one as she tugged the ends of his shirt free.

"Make love to me, Zamar," she murmured against his skin. "It might be our last chance."

"I do not think it will be our last chance, my One," he said. His hands moved to the front of her shorts and fumbled with the button. "But I have hungered for you for far too long to deny either of us."

Lia helped him with the unfastening of their clothing. When they'd undressed, they used the clothes and backpacks together for a makeshift pallet on the flat surface of the rock.

"Do you remember," Lia began as she lay back and Zamar molded his body to hers, "our last time together and you told me about a place across the ocean where my father would never find us?"

"Yes." Zamar's warm breath fanned across her skin. He held one of her breasts and raked his tongue over the peak.

"You were right. I live there now. How did you know?"

He kissed her nipple tenderly. "I had seen it in my dreams. I prayed to Seniha to show me a safe place for us. The goddess took me across the vast ocean, to a new land. She promised we would live there in peace together."

Hope sprang alive within Lia.

"When Mahkul discovered us, executed you, and cursed me, I thought Seniha had forsaken us. I now realize she did not say *when* we would be there, only that we would. I beg her forgiveness for doubting her."

A shadow crossed over Lia's hope and she frowned. "Then it might not happen right now."

"No. But it will happen." Zamar's strong hands roamed her body, creating a warmth that staved off the chill of the night air. "Seniha's promise tells us you will be successful even if we find Mahkul's curse is not lifted when the day dawns. Have faith, my One."

Lia wanted to scream and cry and beat her fists against the rock, but she knew it wouldn't help. Instead, she slipped her hands between them and found his cock, as stone-hard as when she'd first touched him as a statue, but much hotter and more pliable. She moved her hands up and down.

"I'll try, Beloved," she whispered, accepting his kiss.

Zamar pushed open her legs and moved between them. He lifted her thigh, settling into place, and she wrapped her legs around his hips. She released his cock and it sank into her wetness where she wanted it to go. She sighed into his ear as he gathered her into his arms.

"I told you then that you are my world," he breathed while he slowly thrust into her. "You are my past and my present and now my future. You are everything and all things to me and always will be. Forever, my One."

"Forever, Beloved," she cried out, back arching, as she burst into a million fragments, her fingers digging into the muscles of his arms. When her shattered self had rejoined, she opened her eyes and looked up at him. He strained into her and she squeezed around him. He came, a look of pleasure and pain on his handsome face, then he tossed back his head and groaned with his release.

He held her for a while, until they noticed the lightening of the sky to the east. Only then did he withdraw from her and help her to her feet. She shouldn't be locked in his embrace if he was still cursed and did turn into a statue. Lia shook, from exhaustion, satiation, and fear. She glanced at Zamar.

"I don't feel the change coming," he said in answer to her unvoiced question.

She dressed to keep herself busy, to keep from howling in frustration. Then she watched him, magnificently naked, his unaroused cock still impressively long, as he stood defiantly facing the east. The sky turned light blue then pink and gold then fiery orange as the sun climbed from the desert.

Zamar shook his head. "I do not know exactly when the change occurs. It may be when the sun has fully risen."

They waited, saying nothing. They had said all there was to say. If he did turn to stone, it would be up to her. According to Zamar's dream of Seniha's promise, she would eventually succeed in freeing Zamar from Mahkul's curse. But how many more lifetimes would it take?

The sun was so bright she couldn't look at it directly, but by the amount of light, Lia could only think it must be up completely.

"Is it over yet?" Lia asked softly.

He looked at her, his green eyes wide, a smile on his lips. "It must be. I feel no different. Only happier than I have in a long time."

Zamar swung her up into his arms.

"I am free, my One, free of Mahkul's vengeance." He laughed, tilting his head back to look at the sky.

"We both are," Lia said, tears of happiness blurring her vision. She caught his chin, bringing his mouth to hers, and kissed him soundly. "Everything in the world is different now. You won't recognize it at all."

"I have seen the changes in my dreams, though I could not make sense of many things. I believe the goddess sent me these dreams while I was stone to prepare me." He drew in a deep breath. "With you by my side, I am ready, Lia."

Lia kissed him again. "Then let's go home, to the place that was promised to us."

And they did.

NIGHT OF THE COUGAR

VONNA HARPER

ONE

HE COUGAR ALL BUT flowed from its surroundings. Moving with a graceful silence that stole Maka Bradshaw's breath, the red-brown creature's attention remained fixed on something out of sight. Closer and closer it came, its smallish head in constant movement. Although most people couldn't distinguish a male from a female, Maka had no doubt that this was a male. There was something about the muscle density beneath the magnificent coat, the message of strength spelled out in every gliding step, the size of the deceptively soft-looking paws that spoke to her in a sexual way.

Shaken by her reaction, she leaned closer to the monitor.

"I can't believe he didn't see me." Cliff's voice coming through her computer speakers sounded shaky. "If I didn't know better, I'd think he deliberately revealed himself to me."

Maka glanced around the lab, not because she didn't want anyone else to see the clip from Cliff's digital camera, but because she needed to remind herself that she was hundreds of miles from the forest where the cougar had been filmed. Only marginally successful, she blinked and refocused.

"Watch this," Cliff said. "Then tell me what the hell's going on."

Cliff had edited the clip before sending it to her, including adding his narrative, not that she needed to be reminded to pay attention. The cougar had been moving purposefully and all but hugging the ground in typical hunting behavior. Cliff had started capturing the movement when the cougar was little more than a speck, but the creature's journey was bringing it closer and closer and at an angle that would have allowed it to pass within a few feet from where Cliff was trying to hide. The image shook slightly, proof that Cliff had been beside himself with excitement—and maybe a measure of fear.

Suddenly the cougar stopped and swung its head toward the camera. For a moment that seemed to go on forever, Maka stared into beautiful and deadly eyes that turned from green to amber and back again. Although she'd seen a handful of living cougars and had handled more carcasses than she cared to think about, this beast stood out. Judging by the surrounding vegetation, he was considerably larger than any cougar she'd had anything to do with, but that wasn't the only thing that made her heart race. There was something in his eyes—loneliness and intelligence?

Only when her fingertips touched the screen did she realize she'd reached out. Calling her reaction insane, she nevertheless traced the outline of the dark alert ears, the slightly open mouth with its killing fangs, the massive shoulders and thick legs. She half believed she could feel the glossy coat and hear the great heart beat.

Lonely. Intelligent.

Touch me. Let me feel your power, your body against mine.

As if reading her mind, the cougar sprang. Because of the way its body was turned, it headed left of the camera. An instant later it was gone. *Gone. Maybe not real.*

"I don't know what happened," Cliff was saying. "There was no tail twitching signaling he was getting ready to leap, and if there was a deer around, I sure as hell didn't see it. Thank god for this camera. Otherwise, you'd accuse me of lying through my teeth."

As Cliff's former lover, she might accuse him of a lot of things, but as far as she knew, he'd never lied to her. Memories of the three insane months they'd spent scratching each other's itches distracted her until she realized Cliff had closed in on a paw print and had placed his hand beside it.

"Look at the size comparison. Then tell me this isn't the biggest damn cat you've ever seen."

Cliff was right. The creature with the expressive eyes had to be over two hundred pounds, at least fifty pounds heavier than any cougar ever killed or captured in the United States.

And that wasn't all. The eyes. The incredibly fascinating and frightening eyes. The messages in them that even now were arcing through her.

Come! she heard. *Believe. Belong.*

"When?" Cliff asked. The cell phone connection was poor, forcing her to concentrate.

"I don't know how I can get away for at least a couple of weeks. We're so backed up here it isn't funny, and the date's been set for that Montana poacher's trial."

"Do you have to testify? Maybe your report will be enough."

"The DA hasn't made up his mind. Hopefully my findings on those deer carcasses will be enough. How the hell he thought he'd get away with poisoning them before he shot them I—"

"Maka? I'd really like you here. You've worked with your share of big cats. I figure you understand them. Besides, I trust you to tell me whether I've lost it. Right now I need all the reality I can get."

Alarmed by Cliff's tone, she cupped her hand over her free ear. "If I didn't know better, I'd think you were scared. Come on. You've been in the middle of nowhere before. The boogeyman's not—"

"Don't be so sure. What is it your people call cougars?"

By *your people* he meant Native Americans even though only her all but nonexistent father was one. Although she hadn't seen her father in years and barely remembered him, she'd done some research into that part of her heritage. "Ghost cats." She couldn't believe she'd remembered that.

"Yeah. Maybe that's what this beast is, a ghost cat. I, ah, I think he's stalking me."

Just like his eyes stalked me?

Like something or someone called out to me.

TWO

*B*IGFOOT BELONGS HERE. *With all this wilderness, every Bigfoot in the world could live out there and no one would ever know.*

Giving herself a mental shake, Maka turned her attention from the beautiful and seemingly impenetrable gray-green wooded mountains visible through the window to the two men in the county sheriff's sub-office, or rather what spare space passed for an office. The man behind the desk had introduced himself as Deputy Hansen Salcido. So far all she knew about the muscular, tall, dark man leaning against the far wall was that he owned the timberland where Cliff's body had been found. And that he'd been studying her without so much as blinking since she'd walked in. Making her acutely aware of her body—and his.

Cliff. Dead.

"His remains have been taken to Red Bluff," Hansen explained. "We don't have the facilities for a decent autopsy out here, not that we really need one. The hunters who found his body said—"

"Hunters who had no business on my land."

"Damn it, Tocho, I let Fish and Game know. They'll be cited."

"Doesn't matter. They'll be back. The next time they are—"

"No, you won't." Hansen swiveled toward the man he'd called Tocho. "You are *not* taking the law into your hands." He glanced at Maka then focused on Tocho again. "You should be glad they found the body. That way the next time you're on your property, you'll know to keep an eye out for the *cougar* that killed him."

"A cougar? There's—there's no doubt?" Maka managed. "But you said the autopsy hasn't been done yet."

"I saw the body, miss. It's not the first cougar kill I've seen. I know what one looks like."

She hadn't been questioning the deputy. She'd simply been trying to make sense of what had become a nightmare. A little more than an hour ago, she'd driven into the remote mountain town of Blue Gulch and checked into the only motel because that was where she and Cliff had agreed to hook up. Although she hadn't heard from Cliff in the past three days, she'd chalked his silence up to poor cell phone reception or his distractible nature. Although Cliff was an activist employed as the spokesperson by a nationally renowned conservation organization, he wasn't known for staying on task. When she'd spotted the sheriff's vehicle rolling down the weather-cracked main street, she'd waved it down, thinking to ask for directions to the lakeside cabin west of town where Cliff had said he'd been staying. The moment she'd seen the look on Hansen's face at the mention of Cliff's name, she'd known something terrible had happened. He hadn't spelled out that *something* until he'd invited her into his office. As for why Tocho had joined them . . .

"When can I see the autopsy results?" she asked. Determined to Tocho's scrutiny, she locked her gaze with his. Her nerves hummed and jumped, certainly because she was trying to make sense of her ex-lover's death and not because Tocho had reached beneath her surface. Still, she couldn't deny this feeling of what—energy?

"I don't know if they'd release the results to you, miss," Hansen said after another glance at Tocho. "You can't possibly want to try to make sense of the report. It's bound to be gruesome."

"Officer, I've seen gruesome. I'm a forensic expert with the National Fish and Wildlife Forensic Lab in Ashland, Oregon."

Hansen whistled. Even Tocho seemed to be regarding her with more respect. Going by her reaction to his unrelenting gaze, she should have said she was a garbage collector. Maybe that way he'd dismiss her.

It's his eyes.

"How'd you wind up there?" Hansen asked. "They do damn good work, but a pretty thing like you shouldn't be holed up in some lab peering into a microscope and whatever else you do try-ing to save what's left of wildlife."

Don't patronize me! Damn it, this is what I've always wanted to do, my obsession.

I know it is, Tocho's gaze said.

"Have—have you been to the cabin Cliff was renting?" she asked Hansen. "What about the organization he works—worked for? Have they been informed?"

"What was he doing on my land?"

If she'd ever heard a voice like Tocho's before, she didn't remember. The words weren't so much spoken as rumbled, putting her in mind of the way thunder rolls over the land during a winter storm. He was a substantial man, more than six feet tall with long, black hair he'd captured with a leather cord at the nape of his neck. His jeans were so faded they were more gray than blue. He had on a Henley-style dark brown shirt, and the buttons were undone, revealing a deeply tanned throat.

In contrast to shoulders so wide she decided he should have been a logger, his arms and legs had a loose and limber quality. They were definitely well muscled, but there was nothing of a muscle-bound football player about him. Instead, he made her think of a runner or swimmer with a body designed for nearly timeless movement.

He scared the hell out of her.

He shook the woman deep inside to life.

"I don't know what my friend was doing on your land, Tocho." She deliberately emphasized his name. The man was a jock's jock, macho in ways that gave the word new meaning, and she wasn't about to back down. "But if I can get my hands on his material, I might have a better idea about his agenda. He didn't say what he was doing here, but I'm assuming it was related to his work." *Maybe he was investigating illegal activities on your land, activities you're involved in.*

"We'll talk about that in a little bit, miss," Hansen said. "First, I need to know if you intend to contact the media."

"What? You mean they don't know?"

Hansen gave her a rueful smile. "Blue Gulch doesn't warrant a newspaper. Hell, there isn't even a reporter from the paper over in Red Bluff assigned to us. Once I'm done, I'll make my report public, but until the investigation is over, I don't want the media in the way."

Investigation. The word brought reality with it. Cliff was dead, his remaining years of life snuffed out by a wild animal. She had no reason to doubt that the deputy was handling things like a professional. As she did when testifying against the human scum who killed for the sake of killing or money, he kept his emotions out of it, which explained his no-nonsense attitude, right?

And Tocho—from his words and expression, she concluded that he couldn't care less that a human had bled to death on his land.

What then did he care about?

THIS WASN'T A CABIN. It was a summer home.

On the brink of exhaustion, Maka hauled her suitcase in from her car and closed the door behind her. It had taken until night before she'd received permission to stay there while she went through Cliff's material. If she hadn't been able to pull strings with Cliff's employer, she'd still be stuck in that small motel. Instead, after a half-dozen or so phone calls, she'd gotten in touch with the cabin's owner who'd informed Deputy Hansen that he was approving her request. She saw no reason to tell either man that the moment she'd seen the cabin and its surroundings, she'd felt comfortable. Getting away from cities and coming to the mountains had always fed her soul.

Now what are you going to do?

Talking to herself had long been a habit. Unfortunately, like now, she didn't always have the answer to her questions. Oh, she had a solution of sorts that consisted of pouring herself a glass of wine and rummaging through the kitchen for something to eat. As for after that . . .

Cliff had set up what passed for an office in one of the four bedrooms, but she had no business going through what was in there until she'd gotten some sleep. Until she'd gotten a handle on her nervous system.

It wasn't just the shock of Cliff's violent death that had her pouring her wine with a less than steady hand. There was also the matter of a dark and mysterious man with probing eyes.

The wine was already on her lips when reality struck. Although she suspected that, like her, Tocho had Native American blood, his eyes weren't dark brown or black. Instead, they were amber with green flecks.

Cougar eyes.

You have really lost it.

Can you blame me? When's the last time I had an old flame wind up as some mountain lion's dinner?

Shivering, Maka leaned back in the wooden deck chair she'd found at the edge of the lake and contemplated her surroundings. Growing up in the wild and wooly cattle and rodeo town of Pendleton in eastern Oregon had prepared her for a rural existence, but although she spotted lights from the campground across the lake, as far as she knew, she had this half to herself.

Being surrounded by trees and rocks and earth and brush with only mosquitoes, frogs, fish, owls and ducks to keep her company was a little disconcerting. Fortunately, the cabin had several outside lights which cast a silver glow on the water, and the moon was full. Besides, she was on her second glass of wine and the instrumental playing on the stereo had put her into a contemplative mood.

Contemplative or horny?

ever got her hands on the brassy broad who'd taken her mind, she'd wring her scrawny neck. In the meantime, said broad was right. Some of her condition came as a result of going down memory lane with regards to Cliff and the time they'd spent banging each other until they'd come to their senses. Then there was the matter of an amber-eyed man who'd stroked various and sundry parts of her anatomy without so much as touching her.

Get your mind out from between your legs, Maka. There's a cougar out there somewhere, remember? A killer. You might not have much meat on your bones, but maybe he's not that picky.

He?

Straightening, she planted her reluctant mind fully on the cougar who'd apparently killed Cliff. There'd only been a handful of documented human cougar kills. Cliff had spent a lot of time in the wilderness and knew how to conduct himself around wildlife. He'd gotten unbelievably close to the massive male he'd sent her the video of and had survived. It's possible he'd been brought down by a female protecting her cubs, but what if the large male he'd photographed had killed him?

What do you mean, if?

Cold fingers raced down her spine, bringing her to her feet. She was sitting on a nearly new wooden dock with the cabin about a hundred feet away. Even as a child, she hadn't had nightmares, no monsters living under her bed or in her closet. Why then was she suddenly so damn nervous?

Because a cougar killed Cliff, you idiot! Ripped him apart.

Wine glass gripped in her fingers, she turned toward the well-lit cabin with its substantial door and dead bolt. She took two steps, three.

A figure stepped out from behind a mature pine.

Heart hammering so hard she thought she might be having a stroke, Maka gripped the glass. The slender stem broke, shattering any thoughts she had of using it as a weapon.

The figure—male—came closer. Despite the fight or flight response raging through her, all she could do was stare.

The man moved with impossible grace as if possessed of a single, well-trained and all-encompassing muscle, perhaps weightless. His boots made no sound.

"You're here," he said. It wasn't a question.

Tocho. "Yes." Her response sounded weak, feminine, small. "What are you . . . ?"

He was coming closer, still moving in that utterly beautiful way of his. Although enough space remained between them that she shouldn't have felt his body's full impact, she did. His skin seemed to be sliding along hers, his breath mingling with hers, their heartbeats coming together.

Angry at herself for having had so much wine that her perception of reality had been dulled, she nevertheless wrapped her reaction around her. This wasn't the first time a man had turned her on. On rare and unsettling occasions, she'd look at a man and the need to fuck him would become so strong that it terrified her. Damn it, she should be used to this hot and carnal reaction. Hell, given her recent celibacy, she should have expected it.

But this . . . this felt like being in heat.

She'd rooted herself in place and become a prisoner of her needs, awaiting Tocho's command, watching him swallow the distance between them, feeling him take over her space. When he held out his hand, she handed him the ruined glass. Not taking his gaze off her, he poured out what remained of the wine and tossed the glass into the lake. He took a single step.

He must have reached out again because her hands were now in his, and he was sliding them behind her, his grip handcuffing her.

His body blanketed hers, circled hers, demanded compliance. Barely breathing, she looked up and into his eyes, but the night had claimed them, leaving her with nothing except shadow. Nevertheless, she continued to stare, not thinking, feeling, reacting, acting.

Don't fight me, he ordered.

Maka, who'd fought her way into her career and loved standing toe-to-toe with arrogant defense attorneys and their heartless clients and believed with all her heart that animals needed protection from the greatest predator of all, swayed in the grip of the man who held her.

He shifted position, widening his stance so his legs now blanketed hers. At the same time, he drew her closer so his pelvis pushed against her belly. His potent cock prodded, promised, insisted. Despite the fear nibbling at her nerves, her thoughts slid down until she was aware of nothing except that bulge and the message behind it. Her need to be fucked.

Do not fear me.

I'm beyond that. All that matters is you—the language of our bodies.

Night circled her. It was as if the lights had been turned out, leaving nothing except the moon and stars to ease the darkness. Even greater darkness existed in her mind. Only need defined her.

Although she would have fallen if not for his hold, he continued to bend her back. Instinct insisted that she yank her arms free and wrap them around his neck, but she didn't. She didn't trust him to bear her weight. In truth, she trusted nothing about him. But the alternative would have forced her to face the midnight hours alone, and she couldn't do that.

Or maybe the truth was, hunger's teeth were too sharp for anything except feeding.

He arched over her and made her feel small. Powerful arms supported her and she became weightless. His mouth was only inches away, and her lips burned with the need to crush them against his, but he hadn't given her permission so she fought her agony, fought her will, fought everything except this extraordinary man.

Straightening, he locked her against him. Because she couldn't use her hands, she explored his strength with her breasts, belly and pelvis. His grip was so powerful that she couldn't move, which she didn't want to. If only he'd stripped them both naked!

"We're going inside," he whispered against her ear. "And once we're in there, you will do everything I tell you to."

"I-I am?"

"Last chance, Earth Woman. If you don't want what's going to happen, order me to leave. Otherwise . . ."

"Earth Woman? How did you—"

"How did I know what Maka means? Because I'm Native. Last chance. Do you want me to leave?"

Oh God. "N-No."

THREE

MAKA STOOD IN THE middle of the richly decorated living room with no less than four mounted bear heads flanking the fireplace. Their presence had bothered her when she'd first seen them. They bothered her even more now because Tocho was looking at them and not her. He'd turned off the outside lights and then switched on a table lamp which did little more than provide a minimum of definition to the furniture.

"This place belongs to someone your *friend* worked for?"

His accusing tone made her shiver, but if she was being honest, everything about him created a reaction. "That's what he said. It's a conservation group. I had no idea—"

"But Cliff did."

She had no idea whether Cliff had been aware of the benefactor's trophy collection but imagined he'd been shocked and determined to learn if the game had been taken legally. One of the things that had appealed to her about him was that they were on the same side of the wildlife protection issue.

Tocho swung toward her, once again putting her in mind of a stalking animal. She shivered, but if instinct was telling her to run, she didn't hear the message. This man was powerful in ways she'd never imagined.

Yes, you have, damn it. Tocho represents everything you think of when it's just you and your vibrators.

"Take off your clothes."

"What?"

He cocked his head, and his eyes seemed to grow darker. "Take off your clothes."

Her fingers twitched. "Just—just like that?"

Yes, just like that his eyes answered.

"W-Why?"

"Because I'm ordering and you want to."

Heat rolled through her, stripping strength from her muscles and stealing the air from her lungs. This man, this dangerous stranger with his unknown agenda, was commanding her to strip. And when she'd done as he'd ordered, he'd . . .

No matter how firmly she ground her teeth together, she couldn't stop her hands from trembling. If it wasn't for that and her disconnection from the reality of what was taking place in this paneled trophy room surrounded by wilderness, getting rid of her shirt and jeans wouldn't have taken so long. Hot shivers assaulted her. Still in her underwear with the rest of her clothes heaped on the rug, she stared at him.

Do you understand what you just did?

No, do you?

He began walking around her. She started to turn with him.

"Stop. Wait."

Wait for him to study her side, her back, her front again. Wait while he took his measure of the insane woman he'd trapped with nothing more than his animal-like body and powerful eyes.

"All right," he said when he'd circled her. "Now the bra."

Not this! I can't—can't take responsibility for my submission.

Even as her mind screamed a refusal, she reached for the fastening because she needed sex as she'd never needed anything, sex with this one man. Once again her unsteady fingers betrayed her. She thought he might take over the impossibly complex task, but he didn't move. His cock strained against the denim trapping it, spoke of what he was experiencing.

There. Finally. Naked except for her panties. Useless bra dangling from her fingers. Breasts swollen and hard and throbbing.

"Good," he muttered. "Stay there. Don't move."

She nearly laughed and told him she was incapable of movement. Instead, she stood with her toes digging into the carpet while he left the room.

The deputy trusted him, didn't he? He owned valuable timberland, land he surely wouldn't jeopardize for a night of sex, would he? Handsome as he was, he had no need to coerce a woman, to rape.

Rape? No. Whatever happened here, she wanted it. Needed. And he knew it.

He returned, filling the space and taking up the air, bringing life and heat back into the room. "Give me the bra."

When she extended her trembling hand, he made her wait, and as she did, she noted that he held a wide red necktie and had looped white rope over his shoulder. Her mouth went dry. Moisture elsewhere compelled her to press her thighs together. *Oh shit! Oh shit, yes!*

"I'm going to blindfold you," he said and dropped the bra next to her discarded garments.

"What? Why?"

"So you'll concentrate on sensation. On your body."

Run, damn it! Run!

Too late. A million years too late. "Or so you can control me?"

"That too."

Get the hell out of here. Call the cops, something.

And tell them what? That you got naked of your own free will? That he gave you every out and you didn't take it? That you need him fucking you like you've never needed anything? That tonight might be the most important in your life?

Not trusting herself to speak, she clasped her hands in front of her and lifted her head. He placed the tie over her eyes and held it in place while he stepped behind her. She could just make out the spot of light indicating where the lamp was, but everything else had become a red and black curtain. He tied the blindfold tight enough to keep it in place.

He'd been right. She, who had never been robbed of sight, had been pulled into herself and forced to rely on her other senses. She felt his presence behind her and lightning strokes brushing her shoulders, neck and arms. Perhaps he knew about the lightning because he fed it by running his fingers over the veins at the side of her neck. Gasping, she rose onto her toes and reached for him.

He grabbed her wrists and forced her arms back down. "No."

"I can't—I can't just stand here."

"You can and you will."

Of course, the ropes.

He began by looping the soft rope around her elbows and tightening it so her shoulders were forced back. Her back arched, and she wondered if he was studying her thrusting breasts, enjoying the sight and looking forward to controlling them as well.

Instead of keeping the rope at her elbows, he worked it down until it circled her wrists. Although her shoulders were no longer pulled back as much as they'd been, she didn't try to straighten. Soon, please soon, he'd touch her breasts.

Insane! You're insane!

If I am, I don't want sanity.

He placed no less than four loops around her wrists and secured them via even more rope that ran between her wrists. A quick knot finished the job.

"Beautiful," he muttered and lightly closed his teeth over her left shoulder. She shuddered in his hold, thinking of how cougars killed by biting the base of their prey's skulls.

A moan escaped, but she didn't try to move.

"Afraid?"

"I-I don't know."

He nibbled and nipped, and when thunder threatened to join the lightning chasing through her, she started to twist away. He closed his hands over her hips and held her in place. Moaning repeatedly, she struggled to free herself. At the same time, she kept her upper body as still as possible so he'd have access to her shoulder.

Animal or man, it didn't matter. She was female, creature and woman.

Suddenly she was alone. Disoriented, she looked over her shoulder, but the blindfold hid everything.

Breathe. Relax. Learn. Feel.

Her pussy was swelling. Wet and hot, it screamed out its need. She'd been thrust into a black world. The air tasted of him. And she couldn't relax.

His hand pressed against her throat, forcing back her head and threatening to cut off her air. Another hand settled low on her belly, pushing until he'd forced her against his pelvis. Despite her fear of not being able to breathe, she ground her buttocks into him. Found the bulge that was everything. Ached to worship it.

"You know what it is to be in heat, don't you, Earth Woman. To need to fuck more than you need to breathe."

"Let me go."

Again she was alone, her core weeping.

"Where are you?" she demanded. "You can't . . ."

"What were you going to say, that I can't leave you in heat?"

"You bastard."

"Probably."

A sharp sting to her right breast propelled her backward. Even as it registered that he'd slapped her, she turned and offered her other mound to him. *Claim me. Oh damn, claim me!* Instead, he tapped her right breast once, twice, three times, and she sobbed out her need for more.

"Get rid of the panties."

An order, a command, some damn man telling her what to do. Trying to make sense of it all, she stood with her legs apart and the smell of her heated cunt filling her nostrils. Need closed down around her clit.

Defeated, desperate and starving, she closed her fingers around the elastic and pushed the nylon over her hips. She had to twist her bound hands to the side and lean forward to finish the job, but at length she stepped out of her last piece of clothing and stood tall and proud and vulnerable.

And she waited.

Think you're in charge, do you, mister? What the hell do you know? If I wasn't willing to play this game of yours . . .

"Where are you?" she demanded when winning the war no longer mattered.

"Watching."

Watching her debase herself, becoming his slave.

Again she waited, and this time although she nearly exploded from the pressure, she kept her plea locked inside.

"On your knees."

The carpet felt rich and new, and she wondered if they'd have sex on it. She sensed and heard and felt him walking around her. He didn't touch her during the first circle. Then he was behind her again with his hand on the top of her head, and she was trying to look up at him.

"Beautiful." He ran his hand down the long, straight hair she'd long before given up trying to do anything with. "Sensual. Sexy."

Thank you.

"And you're still afraid, aren't you?"

She nodded.

"You should be."

He circled her again, slower this time, the whispering carpet letting her know that he'd removed his shoes. Was he still dressed? He touched her temple, nose and chin, her collarbone and the nape of her neck, his fingernails light as a butterfly's wings—wings capable of finding the route to her nipples and mons.

When he was behind her once again, he knelt and closed his hand over her throat. She stared up at the ceiling she couldn't see. He cupped a breast and drew her back against him.

Yes, he was naked. Yes, his chest and belly were hot.

His cock! Where was his—

With a hand still on her throat, he traveled his fingers down from her breasts, resting along her belly while she struggled to control her breathing, encompassing her mons and tapping it with his thumb until she rose as high as she could.

"Spread your legs."

Another command. Yet more loss of control. Closer to, please, being fucked.

When she'd opened herself as much as she could, he again pulled her against him with his thighs bracketing hers and his cock pressed against the base of her spine. Everything slid down, faded and quieted until there was nothing except his cock hard on her skin. If only he'd let her lean forward! She'd take him as a bitch takes a male dog, as a stallion mounts a mare.

And although she'd never done this, she'd offer her ass to him.

"Please. Please."

"Not yet. Damn it, not yet."

Wondering why and who he was cursing briefly distracted her. By then he'd run his hand between her legs and was bathing his fingers in her ever-flowing juices.

"Ready," he said and released her throat.

Yes, yes!

She managed to spread her legs a little more, and despite the ache in her back, she continued to lean against him, making small circles with her buttocks. He was so hard! If she kept this up, surely he'd stop playing his insane game.

Wrong!

Oh, he invaded her cunt all right but not with his cock. The instant he touched her labia, she stopped moving and struggled to keep air in her lungs. She was melting, flowing into a heated puddle, barely able to contain herself as she waited for more than his fingertip.

Slow, so damn slow, one inch became two. She was so wet that the fluids ran down the inside of her thighs and betrayed everything. He circled her waist, breathed against the side of her neck, licked her ear. At the damp touch, she strained upward. His exploration of her cunt deepened. She couldn't concentrate.

Her arms started burning and gave what remained of her thoughts a place to go. Desperate to close her fingers around his cock, she fought her bonds. How dare he tie her like this! How stupid she'd been to allow him to imprison her!

"This belongs to me." His finger sucked out of her, then returned, burning her channel. "And because it does, all of you is mine."

"No, no, no."

"Yes."

Even as she readied herself for another protest, his strokes intensified. He was right, damn it! She lived in and through her pussy. His cock wasn't in her but what did she care! As long as he was fucking her like this, she'd ride him.

Tossing her head from side to side, she fought his hold on her waist. Damn it! She needed to move up and down, help the friction grow!

"Getting close, are you?"

"Yes!"

His finger became a piston driving deep over and over again, burning sensitive tissues, propelling her toward the edge of the cliff she couldn't see.

"Like this, do you?"

"Yes!"

"And you'd do anything as long as I let you climax."

No! I'm not some damn sex-starved, dumb beast!

Hot friction pumping through her, the cliff edge just out of reach, closing in on it, both worshiping his finger and trapped by it. Wanting nothing to do with freedom.

There! A nibble. Muscles starting to spasm.

"No!"

Gone. Oh shit, he was gone.

Furious, she twisted to the left and then the right as she fought to make sense of this sudden and awful isolation. Her body reminded her of a vibrating guitar string. She desperately needed to put out the flames between her legs and on her throat and ground her teeth so her jaw ached.

"Tocho? Please."

"Not yet."

The roaring in her head made determining where he was impossible. For a moment she absolutely and completely loathed him. Then because she'd agreed to let him tie her hands behind her and would remain like that until he decided otherwise, she sank down on her haunches. Her head hung forward. "What do you want?"

"Legs together."

"My . . . legs?"

"I'm going to tie your ankles."

More bondage and foreplay! Yes. Anything as long as he touched her again.

She'd complied with his latest command before she asked herself how she could ride him with her ankles tethered. But he'd already shown her who was in command, and she trusted him.

Trusted this man she didn't know and couldn't see?

He managed to secure her ankles without touching her anywhere else, and she cursed him for being so cruel. Then, when the ropes were in place and images of her helplessness washed over her, he helped her stand.

Which way was she facing? Disorientation made her unsure and, like a just-roped horse, she waited for Tocho to do what he intended with her.

He began by brushing her hair back from her cheeks. "You don't color it, do you? Do anything to make it darker. Good. You should wear your heritage proudly." He traced her jawline, the slight pressure freezing her. "Were you raised on a reservation?"

"No. Of course not."

His fingers closed on her jaw and forced her head up. She imagined those incredible eyes looking at her, seeing past her barriers and stripping her even more naked than she was.

"Then you've been robbed of a great deal."

"Only my father was—is Native. Even if I was full-blooded, I have no interest in being isolated like that. Why would I want to be a statistic, a dropout, probably unemployed and unemployable, maybe an alcoholic?"

Her outburst earned her a slap to her breast, but she refused to apologize. "You own untold acres of timberland. I respect that, applaud your drive and determination. That puts you in the minority, doesn't it—a Native who supports himself?"

"Not just me, damn it. I employ a half-dozen men, all Indians, which means I've made it possible for their families to remain near or on the land of our ancestors."

This argument wasn't going to get them anywhere. Besides, not only didn't she want to focus on the different ways they approached their common heritage, she was too turned on to concentrate on anything else.

"Some things are worth fighting for, Earth Woman. My battle is and will always take place in these mountains. What about you?"

"I know about battles," she shot back. "If you knew anything about my job—"

"I do. Believe me, I do."

He'd kept her head angled upward during their exchange, but now he released her. Anxious for his next attack on her senses to begin, she strained to listen. She couldn't be sure, but wasn't that a faint whisper, a silken note as if something was gliding on air? Something touched her collarbone. She told herself it was his fingernail, but this was different, sharper, stronger, curved.

Not being able to see for an extended period of time had altered her perception of reality. That's what it had to be!

Or was it?

Acutely aware of her helplessness, she mentally and emotionally followed as whatever he was using on her skin forged a hot and powerful trail from her shoulder to the base of her throat before heading for the valley between her breasts. Her nipples hardened even more and her breasts grew heavier. Every uncertain breath was ragged.

His nail—damn it, his nail—traveled under her left breast before journeying up the outside, sliding near her armpit then slowly across the top. Sweat coated every inch of her body.

Down. Down. Closing in on her impossibly hard nub. Taking forever.

"Please," she whimpered. "Please."

What was that? Surely not a growl.

"What—what did you say?"

"*Grrr.*"

"No! Let me—"

Steel-like clamps closed over her nipple. Whatever he was using pressed against sensitive flesh. Head back and legs as wide-spread as the restraints on her ankles allowed, she offered herself to her captor. Her master. The pressure continued.

"What—Oh god, what is it?"

"*Grrr.*"

Fear and something else snaked through her. Both fighting and embracing the heady sensations, she tried to twist away, but the clip or clamp or whatever gripped her nub pulled her back into place. With this new lesson of restraint and control learned, she arched her spine, letting him know in the only way she could that she'd accepted her latest imprisonment.

Perhaps she'd pleased him because he suddenly released her nipple. An instant later, the same thing took control of her other breast. Despite her fear that the sharp tip might penetrate her flesh, she worked to make sense of it. There were *claws*, one on either side of her nub. She thought of old-fashioned pinchers used to grip and lift a block of ice.

Then the image of claws chased away everything else.

FOUR

ER WORLD REMAINED DARK, but she'd become used to the feel of cloth pressing against her eyes. When he'd ordered her to kneel, she'd protested, telling him she was afraid moving that much would injure her trapped nipple. To her relief, he'd taken off whatever it was.

Waiting for him, she decided that the cloth over her ears had to be distorting her hearing. Telling herself she'd imagined a growl eased her sense of disbelief a little, but when this *experiment* was over, she'd have to compliment his effectiveness in altering her perception of reality.

Much more important, hopefully she'd also be able to thank him for much, much more.

Where was he? Damn it, she needed to feel his hands on her and reassure herself of his human voice. To put an end to this insane foreplay. Most of all to have him help her understand why she was allowing this to happen.

There. Behind her again, kneeling, his warm fingertips stroking her waist. Grateful for the touch, she straightened and then sank down again.

He claimed her, painted her. Using his palms, knuckles, even the insides of his wrists, he branded every inch from throat to knees. Over and over again she told herself that she could handle his next caress. But each time her breathing raged and more moisture ran down her inner thighs. She twisted about, leaned against him, even lowered her head to the floor and thrust her ass at him.

Restraint was killing her! Restraint meant she couldn't touch him!

Neither would she be able to mount him.

"Please. Please."

He ran his broad and work-hardened hand between her legs. At the same time, his other arm circled her, flattening her breasts and pulling her against him. "You're begging me?"

"Yes!"

"What do you want?"

"To be fucked, damn it! Fucked!"

"What will you do in exchange?"

"What?"

He wrapped himself around her and blanketed her with his larger, stronger body. Then he ran two fingers in her pussy so she felt skewered on him. "You belong to me, don't you?"

"Belong?" *Damn this helplessness. Damn this furious need.*

"What happened to the modern woman with the advanced degree, Earth Woman? To the committed career woman willing to put that career before a private life?" His fingers slid deeper. Stole even more of her fading sanity. "Not there anymore, is she? You've become an animal." He released her breasts and clamped his hand over a thigh. The buried fingers slid up and down, igniting flames. "A bitch in heat."

"Yes! Damn you, yes!"

"One ready to fuck? To mate?"

Mate? No, this isn't about forever. It goes no further than fueling and then extinguishing the flames.

"Say it, Earth Woman. You want to mate."

"Fuck me. Please!"

Muttering something she couldn't understand, he slid his fingers out of her and released her thigh. Next he pressed against the back of her shoulders and forced her down. When the carpet brushed her forehead, she turned her head to the side and waited. Waited like the excited but obedient animal she'd become. The bitch in heat.

His hands on her ass now, kneading and patting and stroking by turn. Fingers between her legs teasing her hot, wet labia and brushing her clit. Gasping, sobbing, trying not to beg.

"Spread them."

"I can't. My ankles—"

He slapped her buttocks. "Spread."

Yes. Yes. Please, yes.

Because the rope had no give to it, she compensated by increasing the distance between her knees as much as possible. Her tethered hands rested against the small of her back, and he stroked her forearms until tension flowed out of them. He tugged at the rope. Then, apparently satisfied with his handiwork, he spread his hands over her ass.

"Full," he said. "Ripe."

"Please."

"Don't beg, Maka."

Wondering if she'd ever tell him how much she loved being his submissive—maybe she didn't need to—she struggled to keep the flames under control. He wasn't helping, not with the way he spread her cheeks and slid his thumbs into her crack. He slid his nail—damn it, his fingernail—over her anus. Although she didn't beg, she whimpered. Again.

"We're going to have sex." He spread her labia. "You want that, don't you?"

"Yes." *Yes!*

"No coercion. No forcing. Willingness on your part."

"Yes, damn you! Yes!"

Shit. Shit! Shit! The tip of his blood-filled cock against her pussy. Pushing on her folds. Finding the space between them. The entrance to her core. Gliding in. Stopping with just his tip inside her and his body tense and trembling. Caressing her buttocks and her pushing back against him. *Please, oh please.*

He slapped her buttocks, lightly, over and over. Growled. She became a drum in the hands of a master musician, moving to the beat, feeling the flow, warming to the rhythm, dancing, breath harsh and naked.

"Do you know how dangerous this is? The risk I'm taking?" A shudder raced through him. Before she could make sense of it all, he shoved, filling her and threatening to push her along the floor. She tried to grip with her toes. Holding her in place, he powered into her. His fingers ground against her belly, gripping her tight and hard. The muscles in her lower body clenched.

There! Housing him. Taking that final and indisputable step.

He'd fire-stroked her before penetration, and the act had driven her to the brink of climax. If it wasn't for the difficulty she had breathing, the strain in her back and neck, the frustration of not being able to use her hands, her determination to read the

NIGHT OF THE COUGAR   171

messages his body was giving out, there'd be no holding back. Instead, she hung suspended among the warring sensations as he pumped. And pumped. Between his powering cock and firm grip on her belly, she couldn't decide where one sensation ended and the other began. Lava flowed over her. Its intensity frightened her. Owned her.

Never had she been tied during sex. Not once had she fucked someone she'd just met. In her right mind, she'd run from this man who seemed more animal than human.

But this was now. Here. She bent low before Tocho with his cock invading, and fighting the explosion that threatened to destroy her.

"No choice. Have to . . . have to . . ."

Although his words alarmed her, she was too far gone to ask him to finish. Closing in on the canyon's lip. About to leap.

The hand on her belly twitched. The twitch became a spasm. His hand seemed to be growing larger and changing, fingers retracting, nails narrowing and lengthening and hardening, the tips sharp. "No!"

Something sharp raked through her pubic hair.

"No!" Writhing, she fought for freedom, fought the hovering climax. He fought back with powerful ass and thigh muscles that repeatedly slammed his cock into her. "No!"

Her cry flung itself back on her. Then it faded into nothing, as useless as her pitiful struggles. Her muscles shut down and nothing mattered except finding release. Sweat sheeted her. The volcano between her legs rumbled. She embraced his cock, fought to capture and contain it. Close. Nearly there. Sanity fractured.

"Can't . . . can't . . ." she chanted.

"Can't what?"

"See. Please, I need to see . . . you."

HANGING OVER TOCHO'S SHOULDER, she memorized the nuance of his every step. He hadn't removed the blindfold or told her where he was taking her, and although she felt minutely more under control than she had a minute ago, the energy buzzing through her distracted her. She had only a hazy recollection of his pulling out and helping her straighten. Tears had drenched the tie while he held her against his chest and caressed her breasts. Even as the gentle sensations quieted her, she'd held onto pieces of a memory that had his hand turning into something inhuman. Then he'd picked her up and slung her over his shoulder.

Before she could latch onto the memory of what, maybe, had happened to his hand, he set her back on her feet and removed the blindfold. Blinking, she tried to make sense of her surroundings, but this room was unlit. "Where are we?"

By way of answer, he reached out and a low wattage lamp came on revealing that they were in a bedroom. She hadn't chosen this one because it had struck her as utterly masculine with the maple paneling and dark brown velvet spread. Also the window was too small for her liking.

"Better?" he asked with his arms by his sides and his cock huge and hard. "Being able to see helps?"

"I-I guess." He was so tall, so broad, so dark. So everything.

"Good. Now, sit down."

Nothing had changed, had it? He remained in charge. And she was still a willing partner, she admitted as she perched on the

side of the bed. The lush velvet stroked her buttocks, and awareness of her helplessness and compliance again eased over her. She
couldn't fight him and couldn't run, and he'd primed her pump
in ways it had never been primed, and nothing mattered except
finishing what they'd begun.

"What were you afraid of?" he asked.

"Maybe . . . maybe not being able to see took me too far from
the real world. I thought—hell, I don't know what I thought."

"Lie down."

When she'd obeyed, the coverlet felt like silk against her back
and buttocks and smelled like the surrounding woods. She had
to arch her back to keep her weight off her hands, but that was
all right because this way she could study his reaction to her oh-
so-accessible body. At the moment his attention was fixed on her
breasts, but she sensed his larger awareness.

He had a great deal in common with a wild animal who understands in a primitive and instinctive way that danger is a way of
life. Tocho might be in a room made for sleeping and sex, with the
woman he'd chosen for reasons that woman didn't understand,
but the instinct for survival still ran through him. Ruled him.

She could love a man like that. Become like him?

"I'm human, Earth Woman. Remember that. Tonight I am
human."

Tonight? "I-I don't understand."

"You will. Soon."

His fingers clenched and relaxed, once more drawing her
attention to them. Her flesh whispered of his earlier touches, her
pussy revealing secrets to breasts and breasts sharing knowledge
with belly and buttocks. In the quiet light, she noted his short

nails. The tips were smooth and slightly rounded with no sharp edges.

Looking down at herself, she spotted a long, thin red mark at the base of her belly.

"Don't think about it," he warned and sat next to her.

"I can't help it!"

"You aren't in danger tonight. No matter what happens, never forget that."

Hadn't he said something like that before? Even more important, could she believe him?

When his hands hung suspended over her breasts, she knew he was deliberately telegraphing his intentions. Staring at his strong fingers and broad palms, her body remembered their feel, the territory they'd claimed and what he'd done to that territory. He was going to touch her breasts, but knowing didn't blunt the anticipation, and by the time his palms brushed the tips of her nipples, she was squirming. *Hurry. Please, hurry!*

Yes, he'd primed her pump. Yes, he'd taught her body to anticipate, to want. To need. To worship.

Given his calluses, she didn't understand how his fingers could be so soft. Maybe she was feeling what she needed to and not reality. And maybe he'd mastered the art of gentleness.

The way he pressed lightly only to rob her of his touch a moment later, arched her back even more. At the same time, she planted her bound feet against the bed and tried to lift herself off it. Although he surely understood what she was attempting to do, he pressed the heels of his hands against her breastbone and pushed her down. Then he leaned low and took a breast into his mouth.

"Ah. Oh, ah."

Gripping her nipple with his teeth, he lifted his head. The drawing sensation sped from her breast to her cunt and fed the hunger that had started to quiet.

"Oh god."

He opened his mouth. A heartbeat later, he closed his hand over her damp breast. "*He* isn't here, Maka. Just the Great Spirit."

Another time she might ask if he really believed in the being said to have created the Earth for primitive Indians. She might even tell him that a part of her worshipped that all-knowing essence she'd learned about from textbooks instead of her father. But not now. Not with her fire raging.

"Do me. Please, fuck me."

"Just like that you're ready again?"

"Yes! Damn you, yes."

When he stood and turned from her, she cursed him. Not saying anything, he grabbed hold of the bonds around her ankles and lifted her legs into the air. With her legs now in the way, she couldn't see him. And when he slid his nails over the back of her thighs, she twitched and struggled and cursed but couldn't break free. The sensation was somewhere between a taunt and a tickle, playful and serious. More proof of his mastery.

Then he pushed her legs forward until her knees nearly touched her breasts and knelt so close that his cock rested along her hot labia. He'd kept one foot on the floor, giving him something to push with. Teasing her, he rocked back and forth. His cock stroked her.

"Oh g—shit, shit!"

"Mine. You understand that, don't you? Tonight you're mine."

"Yes."

The strokes quickened, causing her pussy to burn even more. "The journey's nearly over. The steps are completed. And you belong to me."

"Yes!"

The mattress sagged. Knowing what was coming, she strained to separate her legs. Ignoring her pitiful attempt, he drove his hips forward. This time the initial invasion wasn't tentative, playful or gentle. This time he powered into and against her, his strength pushing her toward the head of the bed.

What did it matter? This was his show, his ride! She, the excited-out-of-her-mind recipient.

Thanks to the small space between her lower legs, she now saw his expression. He occasionally glanced down at her, but most of the time he stared at some spot beyond her almost as if he didn't want to look at her. Maybe that was better.

His possession.

The question of what they were doing and why snagged her. Then the burning friction through her pussy raged and nothing else mattered. The canyon returned. She raced toward it, closed in on the edge, spread her arms, leaped.

"Shit. Oh shit!"

"Coming?" He slammed into her over and over again, his chest slick with sweat, taut arm keeping her legs high.

"Yes!"

He growled. The sound rose and deepened. Became a cougar's scream.

FIVE

AKA WOKE TO CELL phone chimes. By the time she oriented herself, the man who'd been sleeping next to her was speaking to someone. His abrupt tone said as much as his words.

"Damn! As soon as I get rid of one, another shows up. How many? Shit. No, I'll be there in an hour."

Although she wanted to ask Tocho what the call had been about, the tension in his shoulders kept her silent. She watched him stand, the movement as sleek and smooth as running water—or a confident predator. He disappeared into the bathroom then returned as she was getting up. His unabashed nudity hardly blunted his take-charge attitude.

"I don't know how long this'll take. I'll find you."

Find or stalk me? "Where are you going?"

"To protect my land."

Turning from her, he reached for the clothes he'd discarded last night. Caught between needing his touch and fear of his mesmerizing presence, she waited with her hands hanging at her sides. Memories of what she'd allowed him to do to her body and mind rolled over her like a fading dream. She knew nothing about him, yet in some respects she felt as if she'd been waiting for him all her life.

"You said something about getting rid of people. Are you talking about trespassers?"

"Worse. Far worse."

With that he was gone, leaving the air empty and her body aching. Damn it, he'd stormed into her world, tied her up and fucked her out of her mind last night. Didn't she at least deserve a goodbye kiss?

What else? Maybe a dozen roses and a box of chocolates?

Hardly. Tocho wasn't a roses and chocolate man. She could either take him as he was or walk away.

"More like run," she muttered. "Run as fast and far as you can."

Instead she headed for the shower.

THERE WASN'T ANYONE AT the small police building. A well-worn note signed *Hansen* on the locked door said that he was on patrol and didn't know when he'd be back. It gave what she assumed was his cell phone number in addition to 911. She started to punch in the first number before she admitted she didn't know how to word her message. Maybe she'd think better once she had some food and coffee in her belly.

The only café on the main street appeared clean enough, and from the looks of things, it was doing a brisk breakfast business. She'd undoubtedly stand out as a stranger, but if she did a little eavesdropping, she might learn something about the community's makeup. And if the opening arose, she'd ask about Tocho.

When she entered, the tall, handsome waitress smiled and jabbed a finger at an empty booth. Once seated, Maka took in her surroundings. From the looks of their attire, these were people who made their livings with their backs and hands. She guessed them to be loggers and ranchers for the most part, although there was a trio of highway workers in bright orange shirts and two lean and leathered older women wearing jeans and boots.

Tucked in a corner sat Deputy Hansen and a couple of men wearing brown U.S. Fish and Game shirts. By the way he acknowledged various people, she gathered that Hansen knew nearly everyone in the café. However, he made no attempt to engage in conversation with those who waved or dropped by his booth. Instead, his focus held on the other two men. Their conversation was serious, their body language leaving no doubt that they intended what they were saying to remain private. She couldn't be positive, but now that she'd had time to study him, she concluded Hansen was at least part Native American. The same could be said for the Fish and Game employees.

"Are you passing through?" the waitress asked. She held up her coffeepot and Maka nodded.

"Not really. A friend was killed here the other day. I'm having trouble getting much information about what happened."

Instead of looking shocked, the black-haired waitress nodded. "He was that hunter, wasn't he?"

"Oh no. Cliff doesn't hunt. He's—What made you say that?"

"Because that's what Tocho said. You want the special? You won't have to eat again until tomorrow."

"Fine," she said, although suddenly she didn't give a damn about food. "You know Tocho?"

One of the older women called to the waitress, but she waved her off. "Who doesn't? This might be big land, but only a few people live in this part of the county. It's harsh and rugged, most of it uncivilized. Have you talked to him?"

"Ah, yes. Briefly."

Smiling, the waitress regarded her. "More than talked, right? Could be I don't know what the hell I'm talking about but it looks to me as if he got his claws into you."

How do you know?

"He's like that," the waitress continued. "Let's just say he has his methods for bringing people around to his way of thinking. It's part and parcel of his hunting skills, his devotion to this land."

"Hunting?" Until this moment she'd been too sexually wrung out to care whether her body ever spoke again. Now, suddenly and inescapably, her nerves remembered everything.

"Not the kind most people think of." The woman's angular features softened. Gone was the no-nonsense attitude, replaced by what Maka suspected was longing. "He's more than earned his name and the legend that goes with it. Tocho looks for certain things in people, things they sometimes don't know they harbor. Then he takes that knowledge and uses it as he needs to. Once he starts stalking, there's no getting loose. Not that in the end most people want to."

"Most?" Her entire being was on alert, a doe sensing something in the shadows.

"The others, like your friend, pay the price."

A HALF-HOUR LATER, MAKA pushed back what remained of her breakfast. To her surprise, she'd eaten most of it, but although she still hadn't satisfied a certain hunger, she didn't trust her stomach to handle another bite. Most of the customers had left, but the deputy and Fish and Game agents were still there. The waitress had come by a couple of times but hadn't elaborated on what she'd said about Tocho. Neither had Maka asked.

After putting money for her bill and a tip on the table, she stood. But instead of heading for the door, she walked over to Deputy Hansen. He nodded in recognition. "I wondered whether you'd talk to me," he said. Then he introduced her to the agents, adding that she'd come here to learn what she could about Cliff's death.

The way the men studied her caused her to draw back. Surely they hadn't drawn the same conclusion the waitress had. Instead, she sensed they perceived her as a threat, but how could that be?

What was it with the men in this county?

"You didn't tell me much yesterday." She spoke as firmly as she could. "Where is the investigation focused?"

"I still don't have the full autopsy results so until that comes through—"

"You aren't saying you aren't doing anything, are you?"

"Of course he isn't," the older of the two Fish and Wildlife men cut in. "For your information, the situation is being examined by both the sheriff's department and us."

"You? Because he was killed by an . . . animal?"

The man's eyes narrowed, and she could almost feel the barriers going up. "He was hunting illegally. That makes it our concern."

"No!" she exclaimed, not caring who else heard her outburst. "Why is everyone saying that? Cliff never hunted in his life. He—"

"He was found next to an elk carcass. The elk had been shot, repeatedly."

Feeling as if she'd been sucker-punched, she stared. "That can't be. His whole life's work was about protecting wildlife."

"People have more than one side," Hansen said. "What they present to the public. Then there's what goes on inside them."

They were wrong! She'd known Cliff as well as she'd known anyone, hadn't she? "He told me something the last time we talked. Something you need to know, even if you don't bother doing anything about it." She paused long enough to assure herself that she had the men's attention. "He believed he was being stalked."

"Was he?"

"By a cougar, damn it." *Cougar. Tocho. Is there a difference?*

The three men nodded. Their eyes held no surprise. "What the hell is going on here?" she demanded.

"What do you think is?"

"A conspiracy. Everyone around here has tried and convicted a dead man. Quite possibly the world's biggest cougar tore him apart, and you're sitting here smiling because you think some kind of primitive justice has been done. But you're wrong. Damn it, you're wrong in very way there is."

"The world's biggest cougar?"

"That's right." She leaned toward the agent. "For your information, Cliff sent me images of the animal that killed him." Both sick and heartened by their shock, she plowed forward. "Technology is pretty wonderful. All it took was a digital camera and a couple of computers and I saw . . . saw that beast."

MAKA WAS STILL SICK to her stomach by the time she returned from Red Bluff where she'd gone to look through the week's newspapers. She hadn't learned much because apparently reporters couldn't be bothered reporting on a death that had taken place in a remote location and didn't involve a local. There'd been two articles, the second elaborating a little on the first one. Although the reporter had mentioned where Cliff's body had been found, that hadn't told her much because she didn't know the area. He'd been mistakenly identified as a lobbyist instead of an activist, but what bothered her the most was that the death had been labeled an accident, leaving the reader to wonder whether he'd shot himself with his own gun, had a heart attack, or gotten lost and froze or starved. If other things weren't falling into place, she would have blamed the gaps on an incompetent reporter. However, damn it, there *was* a conspiracy of some kind going on.

"What can I do?" she asked Cliff's ghost as she reached Blue Gulch's city limits. "How can I find out who or what killed you if no one is willing to talk to me?"

Ghost cat.

A gut-deep shudder washed through her. Gripping the steering wheel, she stared ahead.

THE LIBRARY WAS SO small it could have passed for a storage unit, but at least it had Internet access. Between that and the two juvenile nonfiction books on cougars she'd found, she now understood more about the solitary hunters than she'd learned on the job. Her work responsibilities called for becoming an expert on animal DNA and cause of death, not the way they lived their lives. Now she knew.

Except for when they mated, cougars lived alone and apart from others of their kind. A full-grown male staked a claim on as much land as he needed to survive, sometimes as much as one hundred square miles. Cryptic or secretive hunters, they did most of their stalking and killing at dawn or dusk. Known for their excellent eyesight and superb hearing, they were also swift runners and agile climbers. They could swim. Instead of chasing after their food like a cheetah, they preferred stalking their prey at close range using the element of surprise. They leapt at the last moment, sometimes as far as twenty feet. A single bite to the back of the neck of a full-grown deer, broke their favorite game's neck.

As fascinating as she found this and their physical design which allowed them to be such effective killing machines, what resonated was what else she'd learned about Native American belief. Now she fully understood the meaning behind the intriguing term *ghost cat*.

WHAT SHE'D SEEN OF Tocho's timberland was steeply sloped. The only road in was a mix of gravel and dirt and so deeply rutted that she'd been afraid her car couldn't make it, but she was finally where a reluctant Hansen had directed her—at the site of a small logging operation complete with a couple of trailers. Maybe Tocho stayed in one of them when he was here. As for what constituted his permanent home . . .

Although from what she could tell there wasn't anyone around, she parked her car and got out. If anything, the wilderness smells were stronger here than they'd been at the lakefront cabin. The wind sounds in the trees were louder, probably because there was more of a breeze at this elevation. Except for the road, five mysterious pieces of logging equipment and the two trailers, she wouldn't have guessed that a human being had ever been here.

Studying the wooded terrain, she amended her initial assessment. It didn't take much imagination to picture warriors slipping through the trees in search of game. She wanted to believe that those ancient hunters had been confident of their ability to provide for their families, and their fellow hunters' skills. But they'd known how dangerous life was so no wonder they'd developed a belief system which, at its core, assured that their environment would protect the true believer.

A cougar living in this forest had stalked Cliff. Killed him. Was she insane to be here alone? Why then had she come?

Because Tocho fucked your brains out. Because he's the most amazing man you've ever met. Because you don't really know him—yet.

He'd done a hell of a lot more than have sex with her, even if she was far from understanding the ramifications. Today, with cool in the shadows and the sun's heat on her back and small insects buzzing and a crow scolding her from a nearby branch, she accepted that she'd stepped into Tocho's world.

Her senses went on alert. Her eyesight seemed to grow keener, and she now could separate out each sound. Feeling less human and more animal, she drew in her surroundings through her pores. The land was primal and basic, natural. She didn't understand its rhythm, but she would if she remained here, if she embraced it and it chose to embrace her.

If the man who was part of it touched her.

SIX

THE WILDERNESS SURRENDERED HIM inch by inch as if reluctant to release its hold on one of its own. He was on the closest hill and above her, shade and sunlight playing with him. As he'd done last night, he seemed to flow rather than walk. Given his sturdy boots and the two rifles resting on his shoulder, she didn't understand how he could appear weightless. He studied her as she'd seen a panther watch the gazelle in an adjacent enclosure at a preserve she'd visited. The panther had been illegally dragged out of the jungle as a cub. Robbed of its mother's training, it hadn't learned how to hunt, but instinct had remained part of its makeup as witnessed by its hungry stare at what should have been a food source.

Did Tocho think of her as his prey?

"I-I didn't know if I'd find you."

"You didn't. I found you."

In other words, if he hadn't decided to reveal himself, she wouldn't have known he was around. "Those aren't your rifles, are they?" she asked.

Shrugging, he continued his slow, steady approach. It took all she had not to turn and run. But if she did, she'd never feel his touch again. He'd never again feed her need.

"Are you surprised to see me?" she pressed when he was only a few feet away and his cougar-eyes were locked onto her.

"No."

Because you're so sure of yourself as a stud, or because you believe you've imprinted yourself on me?

Was that what last night's bondage play had been about, turning her into his possession? There weren't any ropes on her today, but nothing would have kept her from his side, not even a threat to her life. "Whose weapons are those?"

"A couple of men who thought they'd get away with hunting here. They were wrong."

"You . . . single-handed, you wrestled the rifles from them?"

"Don't ask questions you aren't ready for the answers to, Maka."

Was he saying he'd killed? Unnerved, she gathered herself to run.

"Don't," he warned in a low rumble. "You don't stand a chance." Leaning down, he dropped the obviously expensive rifles and high-powered scopes on the ground. Looking at them, she knew better than to discount his warning. He'd won some kind of battle against two well-armed men. What chance did she have? "Where are the men? Can you at least tell me that?"

"Trying to find their way out."

"They're lost?"

"They don't know how to read the mountains."

And you do.

He was more than beautiful, more than magnificent. Somewhere between everything male and primitive creature, alive as she'd never comprehended the word. Something sucked the strength from her legs, and she had to widen her stance to keep from stumbling.

This land was his in ways that went far beyond legal ownership. In her heart she knew the mountains were his home, his legacy and heritage and what made him feel alive. And the rules were different out here, reduced to kill or be killed, survival of the fittest.

Could she survive? Would he protect her? And why were the stakes so high?

"Why did you come here?" he demanded.

Even as her mind whirled, she sensed he already knew the answer. If that was the case, she'd never get away with lying to him. Besides, she didn't want to because honesty between them might be the only way she'd survive whatever they'd begun. "I spent a lot of the day trying to learn more about Cliff's death. And you."

Smiling faintly, he nodded. "What did you find out?"

"That people see you as guardian of these mountains. That no one around here—at least those I've talked to—cares that Cliff's dead. That there's a conspiracy of silence."

"And you came looking for me because you're hoping I'll break that silence?"

Yes. But not just for that reason. "I have to know why he died. Can't you understand that simple thing?"

His smile, if that's what it had been, died. In its place was an expression she'd never seen on a human being—sadness, regret, resignation and pride all rolled together. "It isn't simple, Maka."

I know. "Isn't that for me to decide? If the locals involved in law enforcement refuse to investigate, someone has to. Me."

"What do you want from me?"

The unexpected question rocked her onto her heels. Watching her, he ran his hand over the back of her neck. The touch sent a hot and heavy current through her. Images of what had taken place between them last night swept over her, and she finally understood why she'd jockeyed her car over the impossible road. Not because she needed to investigate Cliff's death, but because she needed Tocho's touch.

Leaning down, he curved his body over hers, caressing her everywhere with his presence. She growled low in her throat and kept her fingers clenched.

"What do you want from me?" he repeated.

Your body. "Take—take me to where his body was found."

THE CLIMB TOOK MORE than an hour and forced her to admit that three times a week gym sessions didn't come close to keeping her in the physical condition necessary for this. In contrast, Tocho handled the steep slopes and uncertain footing as if he were walking on a flat paved road. Following close behind, she studied his tight ass and sleek interplay of thigh and calf muscles. Over and over she fought the need to caress his buttocks and slide her hands between his legs.

Even when her boots slid on rock and gravel and sent her to her knees, she continued her appraisal. She'd seen her share of jocks at the gym and thought she understood what it meant to be in shape, but none of those men walked the way Tocho did. He'd been born for this, born and bred and conditioned.

Why?

They were halfway up a particularly steep deer trail when she looked around and concluded that they had two choices. Either they'd continue on the zigzagging path that deer had worn in the earth or they could leap up and onto a ledge. Yeah, right. No sweat. They'd just make a lie of gravity and—

Suddenly she sensed rather than saw his muscles gather. One second he was directly ahead of her. The next he'd landed on the ledge.

Springing. Catlike.

"Are you trying to prove something?" she demanded when the trail finally brought her to his side. "What were you when you were in school, a track star? The hurdles were your specialty?"

"No."

No, as in figure it out on your own. No, as in I'll give you pieces of information, but you'll have to put it all together.

"How much farther?"

"We're nearly there."

Knowing they'd soon be standing where Cliff had been attacked and bled to death made her heart pound. If she hadn't seen more than her share of what man could and did do to nature's wild creatures, she wasn't sure she could handle the reverse. Thank goodness Cliff himself was no longer out here, afraid and alone and dying. "What brought him here? It's so incredibly rugged and remote."

Tocho didn't answer, and five minutes later she understood why. Their route made her wonder if a giant had taken a saw to the side of the mountain they were on and sheared it off. In contrast, the opposite slope was that, a slope. Staring down at the gentle decline leading to a small creek-fed valley, she marveled at what had to be the perfect turf for nature's vegetarians. Not only was the valley full of wild grasses, but there were so few trees that predators would have a hard time hiding. In fact, the top where she and Tocho were standing was the only private vantage point.

A hunter with a powerful rifle and sight could kill from up here.

"There." Tocho pointed. "That's where he was."

Following his finger's line, she spotted a nearby cluster of close-growing bushes. Some were a good twenty feet high, and the ground around them was devoid of plant life, perhaps because the shade was so dense. It didn't take much imagination to picture someone crouched behind the bushes while they studied the land surrounding the creek.

"You said hunters found him. They'd come here because they knew about this valley, didn't they?"

"You tell me."

"I know what you're trying to get me to say!" Hot, tired and disoriented, to say nothing of having battled Tocho's impact for too damn long, had made her short-tempered. "That Cliff was here for the same reasons as those hunters."

"You tell me."

"Stop it!"

Maybe he knew how close she was to breaking because he reached out. Every nerve in her body screamed at her to place her hand in his, but if she did, she risked losing herself. This was his world. Without his guidance, she might die in the middle of nowhere. Unnerved by her dependence on him, she started down the slope to the valley. Then she turned her attention back to the curtain of bushes Tocho had indicated.

She had been standing near the spot where Cliff had died.

Unnerved, she stumbled back and collided with muscle and bone. "Don't touch me," she pleaded. "Whatever you do, don't touch me."

Although he didn't wrap his arms around her, neither did he move. "What are you afraid of?"

You and your impact on my sanity and body. "Nothing. Don't you get it, I'm not a coward." No matter how fiercely she commanded her legs to move, her back continued to rest against his chest.

"This has nothing to do with courage, Maka. You're on a voyage."

To where? And why?

"Last night," he continued, "you turned your body over to me. You survived, didn't you?"

I don't know. "Survive isn't the word I'd use to describe what happened."

His chuckle resonated through her. Talking with her back to him was crazy, but she still couldn't convince herself to move. The air here was clean beyond belief, the sky so blue it looked freshly painted. Part of her wanted to take a running jump off the cliff they'd been standing on to see if she could fly. The rest of her needed Tocho's warmth.

"Are you ready for the truth?" he asked. His breath ran over the nape of her neck and slid down her spine.

"The truth?"

"About Cliff."

Thinking was like trying to swim against the tide. Every molecule of her being was tuned into this man. Last night ropes had forced the connection between them, but she was free to leave now. Wasn't she?

Maybe not.

"I don't know."

"I think you do."

Sliding his arms around her, he drew her close. Keeping her balance didn't matter because she trusted him to support her. It might be the only thing she trusted about him. His forearms rested against her breasts. Trying to moderate her breathing was impossible which meant he'd sense everything she was feeling. Damn it, he must have planned this latest mastery.

But did she want to fight it?

Last night she'd turned her body over to him, and although she'd lost some of herself in the transfer, he hadn't physically hurt her. Instead, he'd opened her up to new sensations and taught her things she'd never known about herself. Brought her closer than she'd ever been to another human being. There were more steps to the journey, some of them dangerous, but there was no holding back.

"Tell me," she whispered.

"Not tell, show. Close your eyes."

"What?" She tried to look back over her shoulder at him, but all she made out was his shadow. His heartbeat quickened. His breathing deepened.

"Close your eyes, Maka. As long as we're touching, it will happen."

Although she didn't understand what he meant by *it*, her lids lowered of their own will. Her awareness of him strengthened until it seemed as if their clothing had been stripped away so nothing stood between the kiss of skin against skin. When they'd had sex, she'd thought she understood the meaning of togetherness, but this was more. Stronger. Frightening and exhilarating. With a sigh, she rested the back of her head against his shoulder.

The darkness behind her eyes lifted by degrees until she was *looking* at a magnificent bull elk. Although it occasionally grazed, it spent more time walking with its great head held high, nostrils flared.

"It isn't yet rut season," Tocho said. "But the blood is flowing in him. He smells a female."

Instead of asking how they could see the same image, she nodded. "I've handled my share of elk antlers. These aren't trophy quality, but they're good."

"Good enough to place on the killer's wall?"

Killer or hunter? Maybe there was no difference. Dreading what was coming, she tensed.

Pushing against her belly, he forced her toward him until she felt the hard bulge beneath his jeans. "It's too late to fight. The journey has begun."

Which journey? The one in our minds or between us?

Despite this latest distraction, she returned to the elk image. The bull walked with proud strength, reminding her of the easy way Tocho had conquered this turf of his. Even with dread knotting her stomach, she rejoiced in a rare image of what was wild about this land.

Suddenly the bull stopped and swung his head around. With breathtaking grace, he whirled so he now faced what had captured his attention.

"He sees something," she said.

"What do you think it is?"

I don't know, she wanted to insist but couldn't. Tocho began stroking her throat and her ability to concentrate started to splinter. Then a harsh burst of sound shook her. At the same instant, the elk leaped into the air. He landed on all four legs and started running. Less than a half-dozen steps later, his front legs gave out, and he crumpled forward.

"No!"

"Shot. Destroyed."

As the elk lay thrashing, the *camera* angle all but raced over the ground. Then as dizziness enveloped her, everything came back into focus. She was looking at a man crouched behind some bushes. With a combination of maddening slowness and awful speed, he stepped out of the shadows.

Cliff!

"Bastard!" she cried. "You damn bastard."

"Now you believe me?"

Hating herself, Cliff and Tocho, she nodded. Barely aware of what she was doing, she took Tocho's hand and guided it from her throat to her breasts.

"This isn't the end," he said.

"Not yet," she begged and leaned into the palm resting between her breasts. "Please, not yet."

"You need to see—" .

"No!"

Even in Tocho's sensual embrace, she couldn't keep her attention off Cliff. She'd always thought of him as a bit self-righteous
with the way he touted his conviction that civilized man had no
need or reason to kill. His expression now clearly proclaimed
that he saw himself as a victor, mountain man and mighty hunter.
Then he looked all around, and she knew he was making sure that
no one saw him. "You bastard."

"You fucked this man. Believed his lies."

"Shut up!"

"Why? Because you still can't handle the truth about him?"

Why was Tocho pushing her like this? On the verge of accusing him of cruelty, she understood. Froze. Stopped breathing.

"Are you ready now?" he asked.

"I have no choice."

Cliff had gone through nearly the same metamorphosis she
had. Although she couldn't tell whether his chest was rising and
falling, she sensed his disconnection from his body. He was
looking to the left with his head tilted just enough for her to
understand that who or whatever he'd spotted was taller than
him.

A tentative and nervous smile revealed capped teeth, but
although she'd felt that mouth on hers, he'd turned into a stranger.
"I didn't know there was anyone around," he said.

"There was. There is."

Gasping, she struggled to free herself from Tocho, but he
refused to let go. That voice, his!

"Look." Lifting his rifle a few inches, Cliff stared. "There's
more than that one bull around. I saw—hell, you should see the
size of the herd I ran across. Unbelievable!"

"Ran across? Or did you call in a few favors and get someone to tell you where the big ones are?"

"What are you saying?" Cliff's grip on his weapon tightened.

"You need me to spell it out?" Tocho asked and stepped into view.

Maka couldn't say for sure what he was wearing, something the same color as the nearby tree trunks. His long, black hair flowed untethered over his broad shoulders. Belatedly she realized that, unlike Cliff, he carried no weapon. Just the same he appeared armed. Dangerous. By the way Cliff was backing away, her ex-lover saw Tocho in the same light.

"I know who you are," Tocho continued. "I know everyone who comes onto my land."

"Your . . ."

"Put down that rifle." Tocho's tone was deceptively calm. If she hadn't been tuned into him, she wouldn't have caught the warning undertone.

"Who-who else is here?"

"It's just me. You and me and the bull you killed."

Cliff licked his lips. The rifle trembled. "I'll pay you for—"

"That animal doesn't belong to me. It and every other living thing here was created by the Great Spirit."

"The what?"

"Great Spirit. The being responsible for the Earth, sun, moon, stars."

Had she heard those words before, known about Great Spirit? Confused and excited, she stopped struggling and again let Tocho embrace her. His warmth was everywhere, and for this moment she believed his essence would see her through whatever was about to happen.

And when it was over, she'd hand her body to Tocho because it already belonged to him.

"You're Indian." Cliff swung the rifle toward Tocho. "That's what you're saying, isn't it? And you think you're on some damn warpath. Forget it."

Tocho jerked his head at the weapon. "Don't."

"Who's going to stop me? You aren't armed."

Cliff was capable of murder? Cliff, who'd courted her with wildflowers he said he'd grown and breathtaking pictures of Alaska's wilderness? Cliff who, she believed, shared her dedication to the preservation of wildlife.

Shaking off her disbelief, she turned her attention back to the scene being played out in her mind.

If Tocho had responded to Cliff's threat, she'd missed it, but there was no denying the message his body was giving out. His gaze never left Cliff as he backed up a few steps. Not for an instant did she think he was afraid of Cliff. Rather, he must be planning his next move.

An inkling of what that move was touched her, but before she could grab hold of it, Tocho faded into the shadows.

No, not faded. Rather, the tree-shades seemed to reach out to shelter him. She barely glanced at Cliff, and his look of horror meant nothing to her. In less time than it took for her mind to process, Tocho changed. What was human about him seemed to collapse in upon itself and be absorbed—by a cougar!

The once-human form bent forward. Arms became legs. Hands morphed into paws. Calves and thighs grew larger and more powerful and clothing disappeared as if the pieces had been nothing more than fog. Most telling, a human face faded. Teeth lengthened and became killing weapons. The space between eyes expanded, and the eyes glittered with instinctive knowledge. Hair flowed over what a moment ago had been human flesh. And the strength in that body—oh god, the strength!

She'd performed autopsies on the bodies of any number of great cats, but although she'd admired their muscles, life had been snuffed from them. This was different. This was life.

A wild beast intent on destroying what sought to destroy it.

Even as the cougar crouched, she accepted that Tocho no longer existed. And the predator taking his place lived for one purpose. To kill.

Cliff screamed. The knuckles gripping his rifle turned white. Less than a heartbeat later, Tocho-Cougar sprang. Struck by what outweighed him by many pounds, Cliff lost his footing. The rifle was now trapped between the two bodies. A mouth designed for one purpose opened. Clamped down. Again Cliff screamed.

So did she.

SEVEN

"DON'T TOUCH ME."

Tocho, who was standing a good ten feet away, returned her stare.

"You killed him," she managed. "No, don't speak. I understand. It was you or him. But the violence . . ." What was she saying? The manner of Cliff's death didn't matter as much as what had happened to Tocho just before he, or rather the beast he'd become, had attacked. Overwhelmed, she studied the man she'd just scrambled away from.

"I didn't have a choice," he whispered. "You needed to understand."

Understand that you have the ability to change from a man into an animal? How can you possibly expect me to . . . ?

"What are you thinking?" Arms folded over his chest, he warily regarded her.

The truth. Damn it, tell him the truth. "I knew—suspected—sensed that there was something extraordinary about you. Your eye color and the way you handle yourself." Rocked by a new thought, she backed a few more steps. "Why did you do what you did to me last night?"

"Fuck you? You're a beautiful and desirable woman."

Any other time she would have been flattered, but right now the compliment meant nothing. "You know what I'm talking about. Tying me up and forcing yourself on me."

"You wanted it."

Did I? I can't think. "Answer me!"

His arms dropped by his sides, but he didn't look relaxed. "Tell me something, Maka. Can you walk away from me? Do you want to?"

In less than twenty-four hours this man had turned her life around. Not only did his ability to shape-shift make a lie out of everything she believed, but instead of running back to her familiar world, she'd braved the wilderness looking for him. Even knowing he'd killed—at least the animal side of him had—she was standing here with her body humming.

"I want nothing to do with you. You're dangerous, deadly. You exist in a dimension I don't understand."

"Then leave."

"I can't."

"Why not?"

Because no man's body has ever spoken to me the way yours has. I've never felt closer to another human being, never gone deeper, never felt more naked. Never wanted sex this much. "Don't ask!"

"I have to."

Her head sagged. "I know you do."

"You could have me arrested for murder."

Despite the awful words, he didn't look concerned. Why

should he when it appeared that not only local law enforcement but everyone who lived around here protected him in some way. He might have cast a spell over them, just as he'd done to her. "If I did, who would be charged? You or a cougar?"

"Both."

She nearly laughed because how could she expect to find answers to something that had never before remotely been part of her world? He seemed to grow larger and more substantial and, for a moment, the change frightened her. Then she realized she'd closed much of the space between them. Knowing she had no choice, she took another step. Her hands ached with the need to feel him. In her mind's eye he became naked, a man in his prime speaking the language of sex to every molecule of her being. Although he hadn't touched her since he'd shown her those deadly images, she sensed his ever-growing control over her. Or maybe the truth was, primal need was stripping her of everything except the coming together of two bodies.

"Say it," he whispered. "What are you thinking?"

"You've branded me." She placed one foot in front of the other and destroyed even more of the distance separating them. "That's what those ropes were about, imprinting me with you. Enslaving me."

"Do you feel like a slave?"

She glanced down at her hands. No ropes circled her wrists. He hadn't robbed her of the ability to see or tethered her legs so she couldn't run, and she'd taken yet another step toward him.

"I feel like a woman. Basic and elemental. Primal. A cunt."

"And?"

"And I've never felt more alive." The admission swirled around her, heating her skin, melting her. Her pussy cried out to be touched and have his cock fill her. She craved his hands on her breasts and thighs and between her legs. She again wanted to drop to her hands and knees and offer her ass to him. For the first time in her life she'd take a man in her anus. And when she was done screaming out her joy, she'd wash his cock with the finest cloth and soap and then close her mouth around him.

Mate.

Only mate.

Nothing else mattered, at least not now. As for later—

"In heat?" he asked.

"Why did you . . . did you do what you did to me?"

For the first time, he looked confused. "I don't know," he muttered. "I honestly don't know why I chose you. Your Native blood and the way you earn your living spoke to me, but I took a tremendous risk letting you into my world. I should have left you alone."

"But could you?" Feeling both brave and as insignificant as a leaf, she touched his cheek. "When you saw me sitting out by the lake last night, was there a moment when you nearly turned around and left?"

He leaned into her touch and covered her hand with his. "It didn't enter my mind until this morning. That's when I looked down at you and wondered what the hell I'd done."

Was some force at work? Something—a spirit for lack of a better word—had given Tocho the ability and curse of being able to physically and mentally change into a predator. Acknowledging that that same spirit had brought the two of them together made strange and awful sense but maybe it was even more complex. "What's happening to us?"

"I don't know." He guided her hand to his neck and pressed so she felt his lifeblood racing through his vein.

"What . . . what about the beast inside you? Can you please at least tell me about that?"

"I don't know if it'll make sense, but *it* began when I was a boy preparing for my manhood test."

"Manhood test?"

"You're part Native, Maka. Surely you know about the rituals youth go through when they're considered old enough to become adults."

As he spoke, his eyes and skin seemed to darken. Although she wondered if he might change shape again, his hold on her was so strong she feared nothing. And because she understood how vital this conversation was, she fought the horny beast inside her. "You're talking about spirit quests, aren't you?"

"That's part of it. Most boys in our tribe were being schooled by our local shaman. I was part of that until *he* showed up."

Midnight lurked in his eyes. Perhaps on some primitive level he was trying to warn her of something. "He?"

"Another *shaman*. He said little, but he didn't need to because he communicated in other ways. One time I saw him and the local shaman together. Back then I barely understood what was happening, but I studied their body language and realized that the old man I'd looked up to all my life was afraid of this stranger and his power."

"If you were afraid of him—"

"I wasn't. Or maybe the truth was, my fascination was greater than whatever hesitation I felt. Although I didn't know why, I sensed that he'd selected me. Once he started telling me the ancient legends and teaching me his healing powers, I didn't care about anything else. I wanted his gifts. I needed them."

She'd been standing on numb legs, concentrating on his every word with her eyes nearly closed so she didn't risk being distracted. Now she looked up at him again. Oh yes, midnight eyes. The feline element no longer existed, it had been replaced by something savagely male.

And the savage female in her responded.

"I-I went to the library before coming here." Speaking through numb lips took effort. "I wanted to learn as much as I could about . . ."

Closing his fingers over her wrists, he pulled her against him and positioned her hands at the small of his back. No longer able to see him clearly, she concentrated on his body. At the same time she forced out what she needed to say before she could no longer speak. "I came across your name. Tocho means mountain lion."

"I wasn't born Tocho. The man who became my shaman and spirit guide gave that to me."

"You don't have to keep it."

"I want to."

"How do you feel about your ability to become a predator?"

"It isn't an ability. I have no control over what happens."

Touched, she stood on her toes and kissed his chin. It occurred to her that she hadn't given him tenderness before because everything between them had been about his domination. Maybe he was thinking the same thing because he released his hold on her wrists and ran his fingers over her spine. Perhaps he meant the gesture to be gentle, not that her spiking libido cared. "You . . . do you know when it's going to happen?"

"Yes. I don't fight the transformation because it allows me to do what I can't as a man, things that need to be done."

Her head pulsed. Grasping what remained of rational thought, she squeezed her legs together and clenched her fists. If he didn't stop stroking her back . . . "Things? Are you saying you've killed more than once?"

"Don't ask. You aren't ready to know."

Get the hell away from him! Run as you've never run! "When will I be?"

"Only you can answer that," he said and lifted her in his arms.

She felt small and helpless, and if not for the way her skin hummed, she might believe she was a child in a loving parent's embrace. But she had no memory of her father holding her, and Tocho was hardly a parent.

He set her down near a large oak with endless seasons of leaves cushioning the ground, and she sank to her knees before him.

"Are you—" he started, but she answered his unfinished question by rubbing her cheek against the straining denim over his cock. Groaning, he ran his fingers into her hair and held her in place. Content, she closed her arms around his legs. Her fingers reached for his ass. Bold and driven, she worked her hands between his legs. Once there, she turned her head and nipped at the zipper.

"You mean this?" he asked.

"I've never meant anything more, Tocho. And I don't want us to look beyond this moment."

"You might regret—"

"All we have is now." *All I want is you.*

Wondering whether she'd suddenly been made wise or foolish, she concentrated on the fragile moment she'd been given. True, he might have cast a spell over her while they were having sex last night. True, ropes she couldn't feel might be wrapped around her. She didn't care. She needed him. Needed what made him a man.

No longer caring about her level of insanity, she tugged on the zipper with her teeth. It gave way as if it had been waiting to be set free, but the snap resisted until she worked it with her hands. Although she longed to caress the silken flesh sheltering hard strength, she drew out the unveiling by running her fingertips and knuckles over his still-hidden cock.

When she'd become interested in the difference between the sexes, she'd felt sorry for boys because their *things* were so strange looking. Losing her virginity hadn't changed her opinion of penises because the young man in question had been in such a hurry to plow tab A into slot B that he'd nearly come on her belly. But as her experience grew, she'd altered her initial assessment. Yes, cocks were strangely designed and not always predictable, but they fit so well in slot B—and in her mouth—that she dismissed any design flaws.

Last night she'd been too distracted or occupied or something to give his cock due consideration, a mistake she fully intended to remedy, if she could slow herself down. Filled with a sense of purpose, she tugged. With his jeans now clinging to his thighs, she concentrated on his briefs. Of course he wore briefs, not boxers. Of course his size was remarkable, the condition ripe and ready.

When she closed her palms over his cotton-clad penis, he twitched. So did she. Under her gentle manipulations, the cotton slid easily. And as she lost herself in her brand of foreplay and thoughts of what it felt like for him, her inner heat grew.

Last night he'd controlled everything, including her ability to move. The tables hadn't exactly been turned, but she loved being able to do something to and for him. Lowering herself onto her haunches, she opened her mouth and drew in his clothed tip. Tasting fabric instead of skin frustrated her, but even as her pussy screamed a protest, she held back. Whatever was happening went far beyond lust between two consenting adults. Layers of complication swirled around them, not the least of which was the fact that he was a killer—at least his animal nature was.

Feeling a tug on her hair, she looked up but kept his cock in her mouth. "You're making me crazy," he said through clenched teeth.

You've already made me crazy. Instead of admitting anything, she nodded and slowly backed away. His tip slipped out of her mouth, and she studied the outline through the now damp fabric.

Don't be a coward. You know what's going to happen.

I don't know anything. I'm on automatic pilot and instinct.

Oblivious to the internal argument, her hands went back to work. A moment later, his cock slipped free. This was no ill-designed element of the male anatomy. Quite the contrary, just looking at the long, thick organ forced her pelvis forward. She barely stifled a moan, barely kept from tearing off her clothes like some creature in heat. She needed this! Hard and hot and insistent as last night, she needed to be mounted. Denial would be a kind of death.

Worshiping the gift she'd been given, she once more closed her mouth around him. He hadn't been circumcised. Someday she might ask him if the other males in his tribe were the same way but that, like the question of where and who and what they'd be tomorrow, could wait.

Had to wait.

His cock twitched repeatedly. He again gripped her hair and pushed himself into the home she'd created for him. Spreading her jaws wide, she wondered who was in control now. *Not you. Admit it, not you!*

Last night flowed over her and created its own mood. Surrendering all thoughts of freedom, she placed her hands behind her back and linked her fingers. Perhaps he'd tapped into her fantasy because he forced her head up and her body down so he loomed over her.

She was his slave, he, her master. Her world didn't exist beyond his needs, but he was an understanding and compassionate owner. He'd tapped her heat and fed her hunger.

Shoulders back, mouth wide and eyes closed, she ministered to the man who had become her everything. Her pussy muscles clenched and unclenched, but in her fantasy she'd always put him first. Today, surrounded by the wilderness where he ruled supreme, was no different.

Wilderness? Where he became an animal.

"Maka?"

She blinked and tried to focus. Her jaw muscles relaxed, and he slid out. His tip was now inches from her, but she didn't dare touch him.

"You started to bite." He still had hold of her hair.

"I-I'm sorry. A thought . . ."

"About Cougar?"

"You think of it as an entity separate from you?"

"I try not to think. It's easier that way."

"I don't believe that."

"No, I don't suppose you do. Maybe the truth is I concentrate on how the transformation sets me apart."

"From everyone except me, because you . . . you imprinted me." Leaning back, she fought his hold until he released her hair. Her gaze again strayed to his cock. She'd exposed it and taken it into her mouth. Kissed and worshipped it. Why? Damn it, why? "Is that the only way you can keep me with you, by casting some kind of damn spell over me?"

"I don't cast spells."

"Why did you tie me up?"

"You wanted it."

They weren't getting anywhere. At least that's what she tried to tell herself as she got to her feet and stepped away. He'd made no move to cover himself, and he'd have to be a fool not to sense her quivering need.

A wind gust shook the trees and drew her attention to their surroundings. Even half naked and aroused, he belonged in this isolated and lonely place.

Isolated. Lonely.

"When Cliff sent me his video of—of you in cougar form, I blurted out the name *ghost cats*. I must have come across it back when I was trying to learn something about my Native side, but it wasn't until this morning at the library that I discovered the meaning behind the name."

"Did you?"

"According to animal totem lore, cougars are the energy of

leadership. It's a leadership that comes from wisdom. Believers follow *cougar*, not because they fear him, but because of their love for him."

"What does that mean to you?"

She, a forensics expert with a career she was proud of, was talking to a man who seemed to have been born of the wilderness, a man who was also a cougar, a ghost cat. "I'm not sure. I'm hoping you can tell me."

"I'm still learning myself, Earth Woman."

Oh god, every time you say that—"Who is your teacher?"

"No one now, but when Pilan chose me to—"

"Pilan?" Suddenly the air left her lungs. Lightheaded, she swayed. "Is that what you said?"

"The name means Supreme Essence." Yanking up his briefs and jeans, Tocho swallowed the distance between them. "What is it? You look—"

So close. About to touch me. Everything swirling around me. "Tell me about Pilan."

His green cougar eyes narrowed on her, and his concern touched her nerves, but she couldn't breathe let alone speak. "Where do I start? At first I didn't understand why he'd been given that name, but as he guided me along my journey to spiritual knowledge, I realized how right it was. He was with me for the better part of a year, taking me from child to man. He insisted I learn cougar qualities and use those qualities to protect this land. Damn it, Maka! You've turned white. What is it?"

"My father . . ."

Grabbing her shoulders, he pulled her hard against him. Even swimming in shock and disbelief, she heard his body's message and responded. She longed to forget everything except bonding with him in the only way that mattered.

"What about your father?"

"I barely knew him. And I only met his father once, but it made a lasting impression. He had the most remarkable eyes, and although I couldn't have been more than five, I absolutely knew my grand-father could see into my heart." Exhausted by what she'd just said and knowing how much more she needed to reveal, she rested her head on Tocho's chest. Struggled to ignore the electricity arcing through her. Sucked in air that tasted of him. "His name is Pilan."

Tocho tensed then shuddered. "Damn it, that's what I sensed when I first saw you."

"I—Maybe."

"No maybe, Maka. There are forces around us we can't pos-sibly understand, forces that—"

"Please, tell me about him."

Still sheltering her, he brushed her forehead with his lips. "I'm still trying to—All right, I'll tell you what I can, but maybe he showed you a side he didn't reveal to me."

"How? I only saw him once."

"Why? If you were related to him—"

"Maybe I didn't matter to him."

"Damn it, don't say that! I can't believe he didn't care. After all, he brought us together."

"You think—"

"Yes."

Yes. "All right, he was tall for a Native. With the darkest eyes I've ever seen. He walked with a limp . . . I never asked him about it . . . and—"

"He'd fallen and hit a boulder while trying to catch up to a deer he'd shot with an arrow." Although her arms felt as if they weighed a thousand pounds each, she held on to Tocho with all her strength. He was absorbing her somehow, taking her into him when she longed to do the same to and for him. "I-I asked him about it, and although my mother tried to shut me up, he said I deserved an answer. Tocho, you're right."

"In believing that Pilan is behind this?" Leaning back as best he could without breaking the contact, he stared at her. Awe and acceptance lived together in his gaze. "Damn it, Pilan's granddaughter has entered my life."

EIGHT

*M*AKA SAT CROSS-LEGGED ON the ground while Tocho stood nearby. Neither had spoken for the better part of a minute, and although he'd been willing to support her, she felt safer this way. Disbelief repeatedly slammed into her. She longed to call her mother and beg her to tell her more about her elusive grandfather, but her father's side of the family had always been off-limits.

"What—what was he like?" she finally managed.

"Quiet. I sensed a sadness in him. Once when I asked about his family, he said he'd lost them. That his son's heart had died. I realized this was something he didn't want to talk about. Pilan never got in touch with you after that one time?"

"No. I kept asking about him until finally my mother snapped that she'd heard enough. She said the same thing about my father."

Tocho settled onto his knees and faced her. As before, the shadows fought to take him for their own. Afraid they might win, she rested her hands on his thighs. There was something age-less about him as if he was capable of existing in two worlds at the same time. Had Pilan come to the same conclusion? Was that why he'd given a year of his life to a boy he hadn't known before?

Images of two remarkable but lonely people reaching out for each other brought tears to her eyes.

"What is it?"

If she asked him to, he would hold her until the word *lonely* ceased to have meaning. But much as she needed to be embraced, she wouldn't ask because she had no doubt they'd have sex.

And sex would get in the way of what had to be said.

"My mother . . . one night shortly after I turned twenty-one, she and I sat down with a bottle of wine. By the time we'd killed it, I'd learned things about her I'd never suspected."

"About her relationship with your father?"

Was there anything Tocho didn't sense about her? Was that what it meant to be a cougar? The ability to see into a person's heart and soul? If so, did she want that? And if the answer was no, could she live the rest of her life with only the memory of one night of incredible sex? Damn, so many questions! So much energy flowing between them.

"Yes," she said and returned his gaze. Even with his cock once more straining against his unfastened jeans and his skin calling to hers, she saw the cougar in him. He was motionless in the way of a predator surveying his world. "She still loved him. I used to believe she hated him because she never talked about him, but that night she admitted it hurt too much. I asked if that's why she never remarried, and she nodded. Then she told me that the differences between them were too great. They-they came from different worlds and . . ."

Although she'd been half drunk that night, she'd keenly felt her mother's pain. The same grief, regret and loss now settled over her. Insanity had brought her back to Tocho today, but they too lived in different worlds. How could she possibly understand what made his heart beat?

"This is my world," he whispered as if reading her mind. "As long as it's at risk, I can't live anywhere else. I owe it to my ancestors and the spirits—and for those who are now alive who believe as I do."

Thinking of the elk Cliff had destroyed and the poachers Tocho had just chased off, she knew he was right.

"Did—could Pilan do what you did, become a cougar?"

"And a bear and an eagle."

Her grandfather was a shapeshifter? "I don't even know if he's alive."

"Neither do I, but his spirit is still with me."

Both dizzy and more clearheaded than she'd been in her entire life, she reached out and stroked his thighs. Friction heated her palms, but she continued because she needed to try to reach Pilan's spirit through this man. And to take something of Tocho to last the rest of her life.

"The Natives and others who live around here? They trust you to protect this land?"

"Yes."

His answer was so simple, not boastful but the truth. "And they'll protect you, won't they? Local law enforcement steps aside when nature and its creatures are threatened. Instead of prosecuting you, they give you free rein."

"Because they share my beliefs."

"So do I. Only instead of growing fangs and claws and tearing poachers apart, I face them in court. Not as effective or swift or final, but the intent is the same."

Gripping her wrists, he lifted her hands to his mouth. The impact of his tender kisses raced through her, and too-long simmering coals burst into flame.

"Maybe that's part of what brought us together."

Maybe, but they remained worlds apart. He became a predator and killed while she was part of the law.

What else was it her mother had said that memorable night? That the sex with her father had been beyond incredible. Her mother had had a handful of lovers after they split up, but she'd always felt *apart* from those men. Not fully engaged. Not given enough incentive to risk her sanity and turn her body and heart over to them.

It was hardly like that between her and Tocho, Maka forcefully reminded herself. Their affair, if that's what it should be called, had existed for less than twenty-four hours. Just because he'd drawn her in via what she supposed passed as bondage didn't make their connection remarkable, did it?

So walk away.

"You could have me arrested," he said.

"Yes."

"But you aren't going to."

"No."

"Because?"

Every time he exhaled, his spent breath tickled her knuckles. Only a few minutes ago, her hands had been on his cock, and they ached to return. So did her mouth.

"A male cougar shares his turf with several females." Pressing her palms together, he held them in place, and she nourished herself from his body's heat. "When the time for breeding comes, he tracks them down and mounts them. They're receptive because they're in heat, but there's no affection. No love. Maybe none of them remembers what happened."

"It isn't like that for us."

"No. It isn't." Not bothering to ask permission, he pushed her down and onto her side with her legs stretched out and her upper body supported on her elbow. His strength gathered over her, and she felt small and helpless. A female tracked down. "I've never brought a woman out here."

"You didn't bring. I came."

"Why?"

"I, ah, I needed to see your world. And you."

"And now that you have?"

She licked dry lips. "It isn't enough."

Her words settled in the air between them. Again struck by his ability to go so long without moving, she slid her fingers under the V in his shirt. The day's warmth had settled in him, and she wondered if the environment would have the same impact on him in winter. She couldn't imagine touching a man who'd been embraced by ice and snow. Neither could she fathom being near him and not touching.

"Your grandfather told me that those who embrace spiritual energy are lonely." He took in a long, slow breath and leaned into her hand. "Back then I didn't know what he meant, but I do now."

"I wish it wasn't like that."

"I've become used to it." Like the creature lurking inside him, he scanned his surroundings. "Nature nourishes and speaks to me."

"Nature isn't a woman."

"No, she isn't."

Although she smiled, she didn't feel like laughing. Strange how satisfying it was to rest her hand against the base of his throat. Satisfying and yet not enough. "I don't know why I slept with

Cliff. I really don't. He wasn't that great a lover." *Nothing like you.*
"He was intelligent . . . and obviously deceptive. Damn it, maybe
it was the deception I fell for. I thought he cared about me when
maybe all he was after was what I might tell him about what it
took to prosecute poachers." Angry, she clenched her teeth. "Was
I really such a damn fool?"

"You weren't a fool. Just lonely."

As lonely as you are.

Distracted, she looked up to see a large bird floating by.
"Eagle," she said. "I've seen enough carcasses to know."

"Alive is better."

Alive is all you and I have.

Removing her hand from his chest, she rolled onto her back
and started unfastening her shirt buttons. It was easier to look at
the circling predator than him. Easier to think about this incredible wild place that had come under his protection than acknowl-
edge what she was doing. Easier to listen to the song in her veins
than face tomorrow.

When she'd dispensed with the buttons, he took over, starting
with tugging the shirt hem out of her jeans. As she was driving
out there and the reality of why she was returning to him hit her,
she'd given passing thought to returning to the cabin and changing into something feminine. But she was what she was.

Sliding closer, he stroked her collarbone with his thumb. "I
can hear the Earth breathing. When I concentrate, I sense what
an animal will do next, whether it's at peace or afraid. But I don't
know what's going on inside you."

"Because we're strangers."

"Are we?"

Instead of trying to answer his impossible question, she folded her hands over her stomach and commanded herself to simply experience. He continued to stroke her collarbone and the hollow of her throat, and she risked sanity by imagining what would come next. Sooner or later, surely, he'd move to her breasts. Except for her monthly self-examination, she seldom thought about them. Being sexually excited caused them to harden and become sensitive, and that was fun, but she couldn't remember the last time she'd experienced *this*.

Last night.

"Do-do you have siblings?" she blurted.

His fingers caressed her breastbone. "Do you care?"

"Yes, of course."

"Three sisters. All younger. They know what happens to me, accept and approve."

His gaze grew in intensity, forcing her to dismiss the eagle. Although she was still semi-dressed, she felt naked. His work-strong fingers were gentle on her flesh, but she sensed the building energy. Where would he touch her next and how would she react?

Would she ever forget this moment?

The battle not to think beyond today distracted her. By the time she returned to *them*, he was running his little finger over the top of her bra. She dug her fingers into the earth then stopped when she felt dirt under her nails. Back and forth he trailed, lightly scratching and alerting untold nerve endings.

Sudden restlessness had her sucking in a breath that made her hipbones press against her jeans.

"I'm not letting you go," he warned. "Before, I used ropes. It'll be different this time, but the outcome will be the same."

His fingertips skimmed over her ribs. When she gasped and tried to squirm away, he increased the pressure. "Even when I'm in human form, some of the cougar remains. And *cougar* is an animal."

Feeling more than a little animal herself, she rhythmically shook her head. Leaning forward, he ran his tongue just above her bra. Next he pushed first one strap and then the other off her shoulders.

Stripping me. Laying me naked.

Wanting nothing more from life, she slid her hands under his shirtsleeves and lightly scratched his arms. He shuddered. "You aren't the only one with claws," she warned. "Don't forget that."

"I won't."

Lowering his head again, he bathed her throat and what the damnable bra didn't cover. Her swollen nipples pressed against the confining cloth, and she scratched him again. He growled, the tone long and low and hypnotic. The sound hadn't completely faded when he yanked her bra up and over her breasts. Air hot and cold by turn nipped her flesh. Growling herself now, she arched her back.

Her mind seemed to be closing down, short-circuiting. At the same time, her body's message strengthened.

Fuck. Mate.

Was that what had happened to her mother? She'd mated savagely but unwisely and then had spent the rest of her life in regret? With a child to remind her of that savage union?

The questions winked out. Tocho was tearing at her jeans' snap. She tried to help, but he pushed her hands away. Too hungry to simply experience, she arched her back and reached behind her so she could get to her bra fastening. The hooks gave way just as he tugged down on her zipper. Working both together and at cross-purposes, they yanked off everything except for her panties. Her heels burned from the ungentle way he'd hauled on her boots, but the discomfort only fed her swirling emotions.

When he reached for the elastic over her navel, she shoved his hands off her. She didn't care how awkward she looked trying to pull off the damn garment. Seeing his clenched fingers and white nails, she knew he wanted this as much as she did.

Maybe more.

Her body put her in mind of flowing lava. A just-freed mustang. A female animal in heat.

Bombarded by the overpowering complexity of what she was feeling, she sat up and curled into a small naked ball.

"Are you afraid?" he asked.

"Of you, no, although maybe I should be. Of me, yes."

"Fear means you're alive."

"Oh, I'm alive all right." She should feel ridiculous with her knees bent and her arms wrapped around them, her crotch peeking out from under, but she didn't. *This is what I am*, her body said. *Take me for what I am.*

Take me.

Perhaps he heard her because he quickly and efficiently removed his clothes. Watching him, she wondered if he was more comfortable naked, and only the expectations of the humans he came in contact with compelled him to wear anything.

Oh god, he was incredible! It wasn't just his body's symmetry, his long strong legs and narrow hips, shoulders broad enough for any burden, the flat belly and proud-as-hell cock. Even with the light dusting of hair, his muscularity defined him. Men, she'd concluded long ago, were made up of disjointed parts as if they'd been assembled from many different puzzles. In contrast, there was a *oneness* about Tocho. Bottom line, everything fit and worked.

"You're staring at me," he said and leaned over her.

"Admiring. Surely you've been admired by women before."

"There haven't been many."

Because you're a loner. "I'm glad." She nearly added that this way she could be his teacher in matters of sex, but he was no untested adolescent. Tocho was man, all man—except for the cougar deep inside.

Needing both the man and the cougar, she clamped her arms around his neck and pulled him down and over her. His weight trapped her, but she didn't care. Needing him to know how ready she was for *this*, she locked her legs around his buttocks and pressed her breasts against his chest. His cock was trapped between them, flattened against her mons when she needed it on her labia, kissing her clit, powering into her.

"I'm not sure if I can hold back," he hissed. "I want this to be right for you, but—"

"I don't want foreplay."

"I don't want you dry."

"Dry? Hardly." Determined to put an end to all talking, she nipped at the side of his neck. Growling, he returned the favor. Caught up in the mood, by turn she nibbled at his chest, shoulders, arms, everything she could reach. Lips parted, he planted his hands against the ground to support his upper body and studied her.

In her mind she became a deer he'd run down. Helpless, perhaps crippled, she could do nothing except wait for the end. But instead of being terrified, she embraced the moment. Perhaps a prey animal was hardwired to accept death at the claws and teeth of a predator. Maybe that's why she feared nothing.

Waited.

"Mine," he growled and planted his knees under him, lifted off her.

"Yours." Staring deep into his eyes, she rolled her pelvis upward.

When he rocked forward and down, his cock pressed against her clit, making her cry out. Then he shifted and found her entrance. Claimed her. Impaled her.

"Yes!" she bellowed, gripping him with all her strength. Her thigh and buttocks muscles quivered, but she held on.

Oh shit! Full of him.

Still bracing himself over her, he repeatedly slammed into her. The ground abraded her back, but she didn't care. Dismissing everything except him, she created her own rhythm so every time he pushed, she pushed back. His retreat became hers. Fire licked at her cheeks and breasts and throat, and she gasped more than breathed. Thrust and thrust and thrust.

"Oh shit! Oh my shit!"

"Fuck, fuck, fuck." The chant seemed to come from his chest.

Laughing at what they were saying, she surrendered to the tidal wave overtaking her. She rocked from side to side while stretching her neck in search of air. Her breasts shimmied and shook and pride washed over her.

A woman's breasts. Dancing to the rhythm.

A kind of fusion was taking place in her pussy, fuel upon fuel being added to the flames already there. She lost touch with her arms and legs. Even her breasts ceased to exist. There was only her pussy, her cunt, that incredibly wonderful clit!

And him. His cock.

"Fuck, fuck, fuck!" she chanted.

"Shit. Oh shit, Earth Woman!"

"Cougar. Cougar. Cougar!"

There! Upon her. Racing over her. Screaming, she threw herself into her climax. It came. Kept coming.

"Oh god. God!"

"There! There there there."

The world winked out. In this place there was no sound, no smells, nothing except her rocketing body. Alive, so alive, she rode the current. Cried out repeatedly.

Then sense returned, and she felt her quivering, boiling muscles. Heard her slamming heart.

Needing back her life and body, she began panting. Over and around and in her, Tocho the Mountain Lion did the same.

She opened her eyes—when had she closed them?—and tried to focus on the man she'd just fucked, but he remained a blur.

An all-powerful blur.

She was in the middle of the wilderness with night coming on and rocks and sticks grinding into her back and her legs locked around Tocho.

Her world so far away she couldn't find it.

But needed.

Otherwise . . .

NINE

"GO BACK WHERE YOU belong."

Beyond tears, Maka reached for her jeans. Morning had just touched the mountaintops with golden light sliding down the hills and melting shadows. Hands behind his head and his body seeming to embrace the ground beneath him, Tocho stared at her. Chilled air nipped her shoulders and breasts, compelling her to drop the jeans and tug on her shirt. She hadn't noticed the cold during the night when the dew should have had her shivering but then she'd deliberately embraced nothingness. Tocho seemed oblivious to a mountain dawn, making her wonder if she'd find his skin the same temperature as the earth.

No. He'd kept her warm all through the nighttime hours.

"What—what are you going to do?" she managed when she trusted herself to speak.

"What I need to."

"Meaning?"

"The two I took those rifles from yesterday aren't the only ones out there. Word must have gotten out about the elk herd. Damn, it was only a matter of time."

"How do you know who's there? You've been with me." *Fucking me. Having sex. Making love.*

"The spirits tell me, Maka. And the earth."

Every time he spoke her name, she half expected to take flight. And now, as before, the simple sound stroked her sex. The sensation made leaving him even harder, but they both knew the truth—they lived in different worlds.

"The spirits and earth don't tell you everything." Speaking harshly kept her tears at bay and, maybe, stood between her and heartbreak. "You didn't know what was going to happen between us."

"I'm glad I didn't," he said and closed a hand over his morning-hard cock. "No matter how it turned out, I needed this. Needed you."

But our time together is over because I'm a woman and you—you're both a man and a beast. Because Pilan's blood in my veins isn't enough.

Leaning against a tree, she tugged on her jeans. Because she hadn't bothered with her panties, the fabric scraped tender flesh. Studying the way Tocho stroked himself, she longed to do the same to herself. She didn't think he was deliberately drawing her attention to his penis. Rather, he was doing what an animal did, satisfying its body's needs. If only she was less civilized!

But she wasn't.

"Please be careful," she said because that was what modern women said, wasn't it? "Whatever those hunters are doing, it isn't worth risking your life."

"What is?"

Don't do this to me! Please, don't! "I don't know if I can be what you—and my grandfather—want me to be, Tocho. Surely you understand that." Tears filled her eyes, but instead of trying to brush them away, she let them track down her cheeks. One more time with their bodies sealed together, please! One moment of drawing his cock into her mouth, please.

And then the memories would have to last for the rest of her life.

"I do understand," he whispered and sat up. As before, she studied the beautiful interplay of muscles. This man, this unabashedly naked man, would live in her heart and body and soul for as long as she lived.

Would it be enough?

"I-I have to go," she muttered and slipped on a sock. "I have so much work I need to do."

"How will you get back?"

Barely aware of what she was doing, she pointed in the direction they'd hiked yesterday.

"You can find the way? You're not going to get lost?"

"Of course not. It's—"

"You don't want me to go with you?"

Oh god, now he was standing and so close that his heat kissed her exposed skin. More tears fell. "Do what you need to. Go! Damn it, just go."

His long, strong fingers curled into tight fists. "You're right." The whispered words struck her like blows. "Putting this off isn't going to change anything."

She'd once gone river rafting, and although racing through some unexpected class-four rapids hadn't taken more than a minute, she'd never felt so helpless and out of control. The need to have this man around and in her was even stronger, but if she took that single insane step, she would drown. Die in the lonely aftermath.

"Will—will I ever hear from you?" she asked, then cursed her weakness.

"I don't—"

A sharp, distant sound shook the air and brought Tocho onto his toes. Even as the blast echoed, she understood. "A rifle," she said.

Instead of replying, he closed his eyes. In her mind, his magnificent naked body flowed into his surroundings. She swore the breeze was whispering to him, birds speaking, the earth sending messages. Wise in a way she'd never before comprehended, she listened for those messages.

And when she closed her eyes, she *saw*.

The bullet meant for the bull elk's heart had struck its antlers and knocked the animal to his knees, but he had scrambled back to his feet and was running. The huge body slipped effortlessly between trees and around boulders. Seemingly weightless, the bull held his head high and in constant motion so the antlers didn't snag on anything.

The image in her mind shifted. Three sweating and cursing men were lumbering toward where the elk had been hit. From their gestures and expressions, she gathered that one had fired before the others believed he should have. After giving the others the middle-fingered salute, the shooter shrugged his rifle higher on his back and started after the elk. A short while later, the others followed suit.

Feeling pressure on her arms, Maka opened her eyes. Tocho was staring at her, his grip keeping her from swaying. "What did you see?" he demanded.

She told him. "How far will that elk run?" she asked.

"Not far enough."

And the next bullet will kill it—unless you do something.

"Maka, I—"

"Stop them! Whatever it takes, stop them."

"By becoming Cougar?"

She opened her mouth to tell him yes. Instead, a faint growl rolled out of her.

Caught somewhere between disbelief and acceptance, she locked eyes with *Ghost Cat*. His features aged and changed and she knew as she'd never known anything in her life that she was seeing her grandfather. Then the older face faded and Tocho returned. But the transformation had begun, lengthening his teeth and adding strength to his muscles.

"Come with me, Earth Woman," he said. "Become what you are destined for."

Instead of screaming out a denial, she concentrated on her own body. Without looking at them, she knew her fingernails were becoming long and sharp. Power built in her thighs and shoulders and power rolled through her. "Did you know?" she managed despite her thickening throat.

"I wanted you for my mate. I needed that as much as I need life. But that was all I knew."

My mate.

The transformation continued, turning her arms into legs, and weak sight and hearing becoming so keen she could see and hear a mouse under a rotting log. Even as the changes took place, her mind remained clear—human.

She understood that if she didn't want this she could return to what she'd always been. She could walk away, drive home and re-enter the world where assaults against wildlife were fought with science and law.

But because of who her grandfather was or had been, she carried a predator's blood.

Like Tocho, she was now a *Ghost Cat*.

"Hunt," she said with what remained of her human voice. "Protect."

"Kill?"

"If necessary." She tried to say more, but no words came out. Instead, she growled. And when her mate licked the side of her neck with a cougar's tongue, she licked back.

When the hunting and protecting and maybe the killing is over, she told Tocho, *we will mate.*

Become one, he responded. *Hearts beating together.*

Yes!

Turning toward where the rifle sound had come from, Tocho began loping effortlessly. Strength and heat and purpose and love flowing through her, Earth Woman did the same.